Children of the Signal

Josef James

Nova Press LLC

Cover Illustration by Peres Green – pyrusplantae@gmail.com

Children of the Signal is distributed internationally by Nova Press LLC

Library of Congress Control Number: 2026910573

ISBN 979-8-9989381-2-2 Paperback

ISBN 979-8-9989381-3-9 Ebook

1st edition 2025

Contents

Prologue

He sits in the bleachers and stares at her. A cool breeze wafts by, and he tugs on the zipper to his jacket. He plucks a leaf from his salt-and-pepper hair. She jumps up and down, warming up for her run. She puts her feet in the starting blocks. His heart swells with pride at all she's accomplished here. She used to be so shy, and now look at her. She eats right, pays attention to the coach, and makes friends.

"On your marks," the coach said. "Get set, GO!"

The runners take off like a rocket for the sixty-meter dash. She comes in second out of seven. She might win at the meet by the end of this year, he thinks to himself. His face becomes forlorn for a moment. He knows he won't be around to see it. After the race, she comes up to the bleachers and says, "Hey, Papa. Ima hit the showers before we head home."

"Ok, Sweetpea," he said to her.

She waved and headed toward the rec center.

An older gentleman with silver hair comes and sits next to him.

"Hey. Didn't think I was going to make it."

"Good to see you. Thanks for coming. How you feeling?

"Terrible. I was barely able to get out of the hospital and come down here. I was afraid they would take this little care package away from me. But you know how it is. It's just another Tuesday at this point. Our last Tuesday, I guess."

"It's looking that way."

"There's still time for you to do this another way, Rog. They don't make the announcement for 2 more days."

"You know there isn't. They'll throw me in the psych ward and call me crazy. Look what they did to Siobhan! I don't want my baby girl to see me like that. They don't respect anyone or anything."

"My daughter went about things the wrong way. But as long as she's alive, there's some hope. This route, though, is permanent."

"It's all permanent, Bruce. There's no going back. They'll never trust me again. And I most definitely will NEVER trust any of them. I see the bag. Did you bring it?"

"Yeah, yeah. I got it. It's an older model; no one will miss it. You sure this insane plan of yours will work?"

"This is the backup plan. If the old protocols are still in place, the expedition should be able to escape."

"I think they're stupid, but not stupid enough to keep the old protocols in place."

"Well then, I guess the backup plan will have to do."

"Back up plan? You're gambling an awful lot on your daughter and an old bracer."

"It's not just about my daughter, Bruce. It's about her generation. Their curiosity will move them to get answers about this world and the government. They will figure this thing out, one way or another. This bracer is going to allow her to tug on a few loose strings."

"What do you think will happen when she or anyone in her generation pulls on those strings?"

"A revolution."

Chapter 1

The sun shone on Amelia Butler and her mother at the breakfast table. Eggs and toast before school, per usual. It's been one year, but the pain is still there. She still hasn't had a decent, solid conversation about his death. Amelia remembered her mom woke up the next day like nothing had happened. Amelia hated her look of ease, like she took the death of her husband in stride. Amelia thought, "Did she ever really love him? Was this part of some elaborate plan to get rid of him?"

Her mother, Diana, read the news on her tablet. Amelia looked down at the bracer on her left wrist. Her mom gave it to her yesterday and said it was a gift from work. It looked clunky compared to the other students at her school who had one. Their's were sleeker and had a more modern touch. When she put it on, a purple beam of light shone from the screen, giving her a headache for a few minutes.

Now that her mom has a job with Central Processing, they'll be moving to the Admin building. The 3-story building Downtown will be closer to school but farther from the friends she grew up with. The Couriers started moving their things last week. Piece by piece, she started to lose her childhood because of this stupid new job. They even removed the signal bar from the wall. A new, young couple will be living in the cottage where she last saw her dad.

She stared at her eggs, which were now cold and tasteless. Why him? Why *my dad*? Of all the people in this town. Why doesn't anyone come back from going into the West Woods? How does the whole group disappear? And why aren't there any security teams looking into it further? Amelia's face flushed, and her eyes turned red. She snapped out of her selfish stupor and thought about Trustin. He lost his grandfather on the same expedition as her dad. Today was the day to start getting some answers.

While deep in thought, her upside-down fork starts to scrape across her plate at a snail's pace.

"Sweetpea? Stop that," Diana blurts out.

"Sorry. I wasn't paying attention," Amelia responded. She glanced out the window and saw Genessa waiting for her.

"It's fine. You ready for school?"

"Yeah. I'm not hungry. I'm gonna head out."

"Oh? Leaving early today? Well, be home in time for supper."

"Ok. Love you, Ma."

"Love you too, babe."

Amelia grabs her knapsack and slings it over her shoulder. The supplies inside slap across her back harder than expected. Amelia looked over at her mother and saw a single tear rolling down her mother's left cheek. Grief and guilt punched Amelia in the stomach, and her knees buckled for a moment. She wanted to say something, anything to bring her mother comfort, and assure her that they would be alright. The nothingness that escaped her lips was deafening. Her mother pursed her lips and lifted her chin, defiant in the face of her inner turmoil. For now, silence was their ally. But soon, their ally would be noise.

On the sidewalk outside stood Genessa Patel. At 1.7 meters, she was the tallest girl in class. Self-confidence radiated off her dusky skin and demanded attention. Genessa refused to wear the standard school uniform and had her father, a spokesman for their borough, advocate for freedom of expression. Of course, the mandate was lifted. From that day forward, Genessa wore only bespoke clothing made by Gi'von, who set up his own haberdashery at the school. He had a select few clients, but Genessa never got turned away. She would sometimes wonder how she got a friend who was the opposite of her quiet nature.

"Hey... bring it in," Genessa said as Amelia walked towards her. As soon as they hugged, Amelia remembered her warm nature. Genessa was the social butterfly to Amelia's wallflower. She knew everyone at school and was nice to everyone. She remembered all the birthdays and celebrations the different families held to mark their new cultures and traditions. She even made sure the proxy kids felt at home.

"So, it's the anniversary. Did you and your mom talk?" Genessa asked as they started walking to the tram.

"Not in so many words," Amelia said, "But I think we understand each other. She knows what today is."

"Yeah, I get it. Morgan has a vigil for my mom every year." Genessa said in a reassuring tone. She is the youngest of 4 children. Her mom went into the woods when she was 4. Genessa barely remembers her. She started staying with Morgan last year.

"Does your mom know what we plan on doing?" Genessa asked.

"Nah. I don't think so. The new job and the move to Admin are a lot right now. I'm sure she has her hands full."

"You think this will affect her job or anything in admin? I don't remember anyone asking the questions we are about to start asking."

"Maybe they have, and we don't know," Amelia said. "I feel like there are so many secrets about this place, this town. What are they hiding that the powers that be don't want the public to know?"

"Or," Genessa replied. "Maybe everyone knows, and *we* just don't. That's a possibility too."

"Who is the 'Everyone', though? Is there an age requirement? Is there something in our parliamentary bylaws that says 'You have to be a child of Kaeldaria to receive this super secret information? What about proxy kids? Without parents, could they never find out the truth, whatever it is?"

Arriving on time, the Tram was waiting. Others got on board for their various destinations on this partly sunny Wednesday. The sleek, electric train headed north toward the center of the town. They changed the subject in case it mattered. Genessa spoke to everyone she knew and was polite to those she didn't know. Amelia held on to the metal pole instead of sitting. Her mind wandered to her dad. What would he think of this situation she's about to put herself in? Is it a bad thing to question authority? Maybe, she thought, that she was being impatient and answers were around the corner? Maybe the only thing around the corner was more lies and deceit.

*****

"If I've told you once, I've told you a thousand times to never ask me again about your grandfather! He did his duty by going on the expedition," Ira Edward's voice roared in his office library. He slammed the palms of his massive hands on the desk. Trustin made sure not to flinch. Not this time. "The team didn't come back. Parliament ruled it an animal attack, and that's the *end of the discussion*! Now get out of my *sight*!" Ira stood up from behind his mahogany desk, blue eyes blazing and towering over his only son, Trustin.

"Very well, father," Trustin said. He rose to his feet from the front of the desk, his desk. The mahogany desk his grandfather willed to him. "I'll take my leave."

Trustin stood up and put on his tartan flatcap. He gripped the inside of his vest with both hands and smoothed out the navy blue wool. 'It is what it is,' Trustin thought to himself. Something his grandfather taught him. He would never let his father think he got the best of him. He'd grown accustomed to the outbursts. This time, Ira spared him a swat. Next time could be different.

Trustin turned and walked out of the office to the bathroom down the hallway. He splashes some cold water on his face and looks at his brown eyes in the mirror. *I will get answers. I deserve the truth*! The steeled resolve he sees in the mirror branded into his mind. He softens his posture and casts a grin in the mirror. After he dried his face, he headed downstairs and out the door.

On the porch, Asher Tron waited. A shy, quiet child, they became fast friends years ago when Trustin stood up for him during a game of Break the Squares on the school playground. Even though he was a proxy, Trustin never held it against him. Tall and thin, he brushed the brown curls from his face and followed Trustin to the garage.

"How'd it go?" Asher asked.

"Better than expected," Trustin said as he paused his stride for but a moment.

"How so?" Asher asks while keeping pace.

"My father made a mistake this time," Trustin says while coming up to the front of a huge, white barn. In his outburst, he mentioned that my grandfather 'did his duty', whatever that means."

"His duty?" Asher repeats.

"It could mean several things," Trustin says. He opens a panel on the left side of the garage and puts his palm on it. Seconds later, the enormous garage opens, revealing multiple bays full of farming equipment.

"One thing I think it means is that my grandfather *had* to go on that expedition. Like he didn't have a choice. I also think it means people with certain positions in the town know the truth."

"What truth? That the lottery system isn't random?" Asher says. The boys walk over to a bay with multiple e-bikes, detach them, and put on the helmets.

"Comms check," Trustin says as he starts his bike.

"I hear you," Asher responded

"Exactly," Trustin says. "I think the lottery is rigged, and they don't want the rest of the town to know. The northern and southern outer boroughs expand incrementally in their respective directions. Those boroughs have the funding and the security teams on hand to do so. A few of the boroughs even merged security teams to reduce the number of people at risk during expansion. We don't seem to encounter anything that the security teams can't handle over here. Another thing, no bodies?" The boys pull out, and the garage closes behind them.

"Yeah, that's always weird to me too," Asher said. "But everyone loses people in the west expeditions, though. We all know how dangerous it is."

"We *think* we know how dangerous it is. Why are the West Woods so dangerous? Not the north or south?

Another thing: the lottery applies only to the west expeditions. But not the north or south. You would think the west outer boroughs would have something to say about losing people every time they try to expand."

"I think you're overthinking it," Asher said. "I'm sorry you lost your granddad on the expedition last year, but you're going to inherit the packing borough from your dad at some point, and none of this will matter."

"It matters to me," Trustin said. "And it matters now. I don't want to wait until I inherit to stop the terrible policies of the West Woods expeditions. If someone cared enough last year, my grandfather wouldn't be dead."

"I don't even know my grandparents," Asher said. "I don't even know my parents. I'm just saying that this is the way it's been for a long time, and the spokespeople for the boroughs know what they're doing. Why is this such a big deal to you?"

"It's a big deal because my grandfather was the only person who showed ANY kindness to me. He is the one who instilled a sense of decency in me. After my mother's 'incident', he was the only person from her family I had left. Now that he's gone, my father is more insufferable than ever."

"I-I guess so," Asher says. "So now what?"

"Now we meet up with someone who has as much skin in the game as I do."

*****

A short ride later, the tram came to the secondary school stop. As Amelia and Genessa exited, Trustin and Asher were waiting.

"You guys been waiting long?" Amelia asked

"Nope. Just got here," Asher replied

Trustin looked at Genessa and rolled his eyes.

"Take it in Number Two. I bet you'll study harder next time," Genessa teases, referring to the Mathageddon challenge she just won.

"Anyway..." Trustin said, starting to ignore Genessa. He and Genessa had known each other since they were kids. But Trustin hated losing, and this loss felt like an itch he couldn't scratch.

"Things with my dad were a bust. He's not greenlighting anything involving minors. He's especially not greenlighting a trip into the West Woods. I'm sure he's not even going to present it to Parliament. He did, however, say that my grandfather did his duty and that the team not coming back was ruled an animal attack."

"An animal attack," Amelia asked, perplexed. "The colony seeded this planet with prey animals when they got here. The predatory animals are few and far between."

"Don't I know it," Trustin said. "So it's time to move on to plan B. Let's meet in Sirius Park after school and figure out a strategy. Somehow, we are going to get to the bottom of this."

As the group headed into the school, an announcement came through the signal bars on campus:

"Attention, citizens of Kaeldaria. A new expedition is scheduled to depart in three days. The lottery system has made its selection, and the chosen citizens have been notified. Congratulations! Thank you for your service as citizens of Kaeldaria."

A light tone closed out the announcement, and the group looked at each other.

"I think we are out of time," Amelia said.

Chapter 2

Sirius Park is located just south of the school, closer to Amelia and Genessa's respective boroughs. Covering a square kilometer, the park boasted an indoor and outdoor facility. Children from secondary would play and exercise there in between classes or after school. The park had the usual trappings of a school; the interior recreation center housed the smaller basketball and volleyball courts. The exterior was where soccer, rugby, and track were, along with a signal bar on a pole.

Because it was in the Water Reclamation Borough across town, Trustin and Asher rode E-bikes there to save time. Amelia and Genessa live closer to the park so that they can walk. Both changed out of their school uniforms into more comfortable cotton shirts and pants. Trustin and Asher didn't have time to change because of the distance. The girls started walking towards the bleachers. Trustin and Asher followed suit. Now they could talk without interruption.

"Well, do we think we can get a spokesperson on our side if Trustin's dad flat out rejected the idea?" Amelia asked.

"Since we had the entire day go by before we could even talk to anyone, I'm sure my father has poisoned the well," Trustin replies. "We can try to talk to more people we might trust or those who are in positions of some importance, but they'll probably fob us off as well."

"What should we do to convince them that this is important?" Genessa asks. "We need some way to get answers."

"I think the answers are inside the town and outside the town," Amelia says. "We need to talk to more people and try to gauge their temperature about minors going into the West Woods."

"How so?" Trustin asks, folding his arms.

"Well," Amelia began, "If we ask other people about the West Woods, they should have an opinion. Many people have lost family and friends in the expeditions. They have to be curious, right? They have to have done *some* investigating of their loved ones' deaths, right?

Doesn't that make sense? We can't be the only ones to have thought this. Maybe we can piggyback on someone else's investigation. That would help a lot."

"With my father now aware," Trustin replied, "I don't think we are going to be able to pull that off. We need more of a direct approach."

Genessa turns her gaze toward Trustin, and her face starts to lose color in anticipation of the words he says next.

"We need to break through the west gate and explore the woods ourselves," Trustin declared. "The time for getting permission is over. I want answers!" Trustin's face started to become flush. His jawline was rendered taut by the gnashing of his teeth.

Genessa cocked her head in bewilderment. "Are you insane?!" she blurts out. "We aren't trained for that type of thing! We know factually that those who go into the West Woods don't come back! That means if we go into the West Woods, WE aren't coming back! How can we get evidence and bring it in front of *anyone* if we're *dead*!?" Genessa blurted out while flailing her hands.

"If there are dead bodies in the woods," Trustin yelled, "Then that means there's evidence of what's happening! Evidence that we need to reach out to other people in the town so we can create change in the system!"

"Genessa's right," Amelia said while she stared into space. "We have to think this through more. We can't just randomly cross into the West Woods. We would need gear, have to sneak out, keep trackers on us..."

"Are you actually considering this?" Genessa yells at Amelia. "Wake up, people! We cannot go into the West Woods! It's a suicide mission! OK. OK. I'm outta here." Genessa said while walking off the bleachers.

Trustin stares at Genessa while she walks away.

"Is she going to get someone to contend against us?" Trustin asked

"She'll come around," Amelia said. "She knows we're onto something, and she likes gossip. The danger part is real, though. We need to figure out how to get this done as safely as possible."

"If we are playing it safe, for now, let's go with your idea; talk to some of the spokespeople and feel them out. You have an idea of who we should talk to specifically?"

"Hmm... We are still moving. I can talk to Mr. Maclachlan. Maybe Ms. Wells, too. You live close to Ms.

Wainwright. Her husband was on the expedition with my dad and your grandfather. She should have plenty to say about it."

"Yeah. She *should*. Let's find out. Are you able to talk to Ms. Wainwright, Asher?" Trustin asked.

"Um, I'm not good with people like that," Asher said. "I can go to the library with the twins and research the origins of the town. We can cover more ground that way, and they would never pass up a chance to go to the library."

"Oh, that's a good point, Asher," Amelia said. "Thanks. Let's meet tomorrow after we get more info."

"Check it out," Asher said while pointing to the rec center. "Ms. Wells just went inside."

"Hmm...." Amelia said to herself. "Nah, I'm heading home. I need to talk to my ma about this, too."

"Where are we meeting up? Here again?" Trustin asked

"No," Amelia said. "We should meet up at Morgan's tomorrow. She will have some answers for sure."

"Uh, is Genessa going to be cool with you talking to her sister?" Asher asked.

"Maybe, maybe not," Amelia replied. "But Morgan just got a job at the Security Borough. She might be able to help us out with something."

*****

Everyone who worked in the Admin Borough lived in the same buildings. The borough was the smallest and was located near the center of the town. It was one of the few buildings that needed an elevator. The new apartment for the Butler family was located on the 5th floor, just a few doors from the elevator. Amelia glanced at the empty bracket in the living room where the new signal bar would be installed.

"Thanks for doing this, Ma," Amelia said as she came into the living room.

"You're welcome, Sweetpea," Diana said.

Amelia had just gotten done drying her giant head of hair. Coarse and rebellious, it looked like it adamantly defied the laws of gravity. The new apartment in the Admin borough would take some getting used to. Amelia looked in the kitchen and saw the pestle and mortar set her mother used was stained purple.

"Oh, did you make your purple moisturizer for me?" Amelia said excitedly.

"I sure did," Diana said. "It makes the new place smell good, too."

"Yeah, it does. What's in it this time? Smells like more Lavender."

"One part Jojoba, one part Aloe, and 2 parts Lavender."

Amelia sat on the floor between her mother's legs, facing the new viewscreen that was in the living room. The news was on, but they had it muted. Diana had a bowl full of the purple moisturizer, which was neither solid nor liquid, on the left side of the couch. She had a comb on a towel on the right side of the couch. She took some of the substance and dabbed it generously into sections of Amelia's hair.

"I'm glad we were able to keep the couch," Amelia said. "Sometimes the Couriers give your furniture away to a newer family without even telling you."

"Your dad made this couch right after we got married. I'm not ready to part with it just yet."

Amelia's head bowed down, still holding the weight of grief.

"I miss him, too, Sweetpea. You know, there's a lot we never got to tell you. We thought we would have more time. Funny how that works."

"Tell me what?"

"Well, for starters, had you ever asked yourself why your dad was so much older than me?"

"Uh, I guess not. I never really thought about it."

"Your dad was 15 years older than me."

"Really?"

"Yup. We met at the annual textile borough function that the spokespeople put on every year for their Boroughs. I thought he was handsome, but I didn't know he was that much older. We started talking, and he said he was a widower."

"What?! Daddy was married before?"

"Yeah, he was. He was a spokesperson, too. For the tech borough. He was a great engineer."

"What happened?"

"There was a fire, and his wife and son died. He said he could never go back to that house. So he retired from being a spokesperson and moved to the textile district. He had been in the textile borough for 3 years before he decided to attend the annual function. I knew someone had joined the borough, but I wasn't trying to be in anybody's business."

"Aw, I had a brother I didn't get to meet."

"We felt bad but didn't know how or when to tell you."

"Wait, Genessa's dad is the spokesperson of that borough now."

"Yup, he stepped up after your dad left."

"How did he wind up making furniture?"

"He was a fabricator; he was used to taking things and putting them together. He knew how to make the frame that he wanted, but Tim McLachlan helped him put on the material."

"Oh yeah, that reminds me, I need to talk to Mr. McLachlan."

"Bout what, Sweetpea?" Diana asked.

"Some of us want to know about the West Woods; why they're so dangerous and what we can do to make them safer going forward."

"What do you think we can do?"

"Well, for starters, why aren't people properly armed? I'm not a weapon specialist, but it seems like the

Outer Boroughs don't have issues expanding their land. Those are the biggest boroughs."

"They need a lot of land for the food they produce. Your friend, Trustin, lives in the Meatpacking Borough. The colony's meat comes from their sheep, goats, and chickens."

"Right, I get that. I'm just saying that only the West Woods seem to have a danger issue."

"Well, like your dad would say, 'Talk it out.'"

"Ok, so, this is what it looks like to me; all the Outer Boroughs have security forces, right? But when was the last time we heard anything about them getting hurt or killed when they explore outside the perimeter? Hardly ever. And after all this time, whatever is dangerous in the woods would have spread, wouldn't it?"

"Hmm, maybe," Diana said while continuing a fourth braid. "Sounds like good questions to ask Tim. Maybe some things will start to change around here."

"I hope I can start that change. I don't want anyone else to go through what we went through."

*****

The small, quaint home was a perfect size for a widow. Trustin inhaled the smell of fresh blue paint. Ms.

Wainwright just moved in, a year to the day of losing her husband. Trustin could smell fresh wood, too. A different signal device was installed in this home than in her last place, where she raised her kids. It glowed green and had a constant hum.

Trustin sat in an upholstered chair that seemed too big for his frame. He leaned forward with his elbows on his knees and his fingers interlocked while he listened to his host.

"Well, nothing happened out of the ordinary, I suppose." Ms. Wainwright said. She was always a kind woman to the children in the neighborhood. She was in her mid-50's and had 2 children: Wyatt and Wilson. Her sons were close in age, in sixth form, and stayed on campus. Her husband was a part of the last expedition to the West Woods with Trustin's grandfather.

"The news came through the signal, as it does, and we knew what to do. He said it was his duty as a citizen of Kaeldaria to support the expedition into the woods."

"He was joined by Mr. McGregor, my grandfather, Mr. Butler, Ms. Boxler, Ms. Dubois, and Ms. Lattice," Trustin mentioned. "As far as I can remember. There may have been more, but I'll need to look up more info.

Was there anything that these people had in common that you knew of? Had they been in the hospital recently? Similar allergies, genetic issues, or anything like that?"

"I remember they were all in the same graduating class of '42. I just started secondary school that year. I wasn't really close with them because of the age gap. When there was a mixer in my 20's, that's when I met Randall."

"Did you know other similarities from past expedition groups?"

"Well, I remember my father saying something similar to Randall; that it was his duty as a citizen of Kaeldaria to assist with the expedition."

"Is that a common expression, 'duty as a citizen of Kaeldaria'"?

"I think everyone says it when their turn comes."

"What do you mean when their turn comes?"

"Well, I can't remember the last time someone died a natural death. Can you? If you don't get sick, most other people of Kaeldaria get lost in the woods at some point or another."

Trustin thought about the truthfulness of the statement, and a chill ran through his bones.

*****

"Have you spoken about this with anyone else, Amelia?" Ms. Wells asked. "Your mother, perhaps?" Ms. Wells, the school principal, often spoke in a sickeningly sweet tone. Having that tone now made Amelia disgusted.

"No, Ms. Wells," Amelia fixed her face, as her father taught her. 'Never let them see you sweat,' he would say. "This week is the anniversary of the expedition my father was a part of. My mom is in the middle of our move to the Admin Borough. I know she has some important work to do, so I didn't bring it up to her yet." Amelia tried to look sad, but deep inside, a rage started to brew.

"I know the same things that you do, Amelia; a group went to explore the West Woods and didn't return. The government officials ruled it an animal attack."

"Why don't we ever go find evidence of those attacks?" Amelia asked. "When there's a murder in town, you need evidence for that. When anything dangerous or illegal happens in town, you need evidence. Evidence only matters in town?"

"Those are good questions, Amelia." Ms. Wells' tone shifted. Amelia pretended not to notice. "Maybe you should talk to Mr. Maclachlan. Isn't he the spokesperson for your old borough?"

"Yes, he is. Have other students brought this subject up? Am I the only one?"

"We need to explore the woods to expand our territory so our town can grow. However, we also know that the woods are dangerous. Most students accept that. I'm sorry your father was lost in the West Woods expedition. I have a great many pieces of clothing that he helped me preserve. He was a good man, and talent like his was one-of-a-kind."

"But why was my father chosen? He didn't have any knowledge of what to do in the woods."

"Your father loved this community. When the government calls us to a task, we should accept it. Your father understood that. If he didn't go, someone else would have. How would you feel if your father didn't accept his assignment and then someone else went in his place?

"I don't know..." Amelia's voice trailed off. "Why don't they have criminals go? If the news on the wave is always saying 'resources are scarce', why keep people around who want to break those rules? Why put hard-working people with families at risk? It doesn't make sense."

"It is a very harsh world we live in, Amelia. You know this. That's why your studies are important. You want to ensure your contributions to this community have meaning. Make sure that you study hard and apply for positions that will allow you to make positive changes. Meanwhile, talk to Mr. Maclachlan. Maybe he can help."

"That's fair, Ms. Wells. Thanks for hearing me out."

*****

Amelia rings the bell of the colonial-style mansion. It had white-washed stone pillars. The mansion was accented with a cerulean blue. The servant answered the door and guided her into the foyer. Mr. Maclachlan met her at the entrance of the living room.

Timothy Maclachlan was the spokesperson for the Textile Borough for all of Amelia's life. He was a portly, pale man with sky blue eyes and white hair. Since her father was the best fabricator in the borough, He would come over for tea and chat about business and the neighborhood.

"How are your new digs, hmm? Your mother's promotion has moved you closer to the downtown area, yes?"

"We're still moving in. It's smaller than living here in the textile borough, but all the things we need are closer to home."

"Would you kindly have a spot of tea?" Mr. Maclachlan asked.

"Oh no, I'm fine, thank you, Mr. Maclachlan," Amelia responded.

"You say this is for a history project?" Mr. Maclachlan asked Amelia as they walked to the living room. Amelia saw the signal bar in the corner of the Living Room. She took a mental note of the colors. His bar's green light was on, but he had a purple light on the far right of the bar that was off.

"Well, we have history projects next year, and I'm just getting a jump on the assignment. Mr. Maclachlan, don't you think –"

"Just call me Tim," Mr. Maclachlan said. "Your family has been a part of this borough your whole life; there's no need to stand on formalities with me. I miss having someone like your father around, you know. Good help really is hard to find."

Mr. Maclachlan waves to his servant, who brought him some tea. He and Amelia have a seat in the living room. She sits on the lush, leather sofa, and he sits across from her in a club chair, balancing his tea on a saucer.

"Well, Tim, as part of my assignment, I wanted to know more about the expeditions into the woods. The expeditions that go out west have a 100% failure rate. No equipment or bodies are ever recovered. Have there been any attempts to recover something?"

"Oh, well, I'm not really over that department. That's more of a Security Borough question. To your point, though, there are dangers out there that we haven't figured out yet. Oh, it could be viral or bacterial, wild animals, or some such that we've never encountered before that doesn't like humans. The original colony that landed here picked this world because the surveys said it was safe. Well, safe enough anyway. Nothing is 100% certain when it comes to space exploration."

"Yeah, that makes sense," Amelia said with an agreeable tone. "The thing is, the spokespersons on the north side of town don't seem to have an issue with their expansion. The Edward, William, and Charles families can expand their borders just fine. They must be doing something right. But it seems like the protocol for the West Woods expeditions is flawed in some way. Is there a way to change that?"

"Oh, you could ask one of the spokespersons for the border boroughs. There may be some geological issues that impede their progress."

Tim rubs the rim of his teacup with his middle finger. A small, familiar hum emits from it.

"Would you kindly have a spot of tea?" He asked again.

"No, no, I'm ok."

Tim starts to stroke his snow-white beard.

"But of all the things to do a project on, why this? It seems like a topic that's too close to home. I know I didn't want to talk about the woods when I lost my mother and father."

Amelia swallows the jagged, patronizing words and presses further.

"I'm interested in the expeditions and the woods *because* I lost my father to them. If there is a way to make the woods safer or better understand why we have so many losses from this particular entrance into the woods, maybe we could make some changes."

"Oh, safety issues are definitely a security borough concern. If you talk to the border boroughs, you can see what their procedure is for land annexation. All expansion to the west goes through the Security Borough."

Tim starts to shuffle uncomfortably in his seat.

"Well, I do have some other priorities that need attending to. Sorry, I couldn't be of more assistance."

"You have been of great assistance, Tim. Thank you for your time."

Tim sees Amelia out. After he closes the door, he goes to a panel underneath the signal bar in the living room. He touches it, and the panel slides up. He pushes a button and states, "Emergency meeting needed. The Butler child is broken and needs to be fixed. Repeat: The Butler child is broken and needs to be fixed."

Chapter 3

Tron House is located on the Southwest side of the town, in the Mining Borough. In a Brownstone building, all proxy children were sent to Tron House after birth. There were currently eleven children living in Tron House, and it was always run by a "Ms. Tron". All the children had the last name Tron to identify them in the community better.

Asher opens the door and greets his siblings. Some are dancing or playing games. The twins, though, he knew where they would be. He looks at the ceiling and hears the bumping and tussling of furniture. He headed upstairs.

As he made his way to the east bedroom, he heard yelling and fighting. He opened the door to find 2 pre-teen boys wrestling. The bedroom held bunk beds, a desk with a computer and a viewscreen, and mats on the padded floor. By the window was a telescope. Eli and Abel Tron were closer to each other than the other proxy children. Even though they look nothing alike, everyone called them 'twins' because they were born on the same day.

"Hey, stupids. Get dressed." Asher said.

Eli had Abel in a headlock, mimicking the wrestling move shown on the computer's viewscreen.

"Where are we going?" Eli asked while releasing Abel.

"To the library. I need to get some research done about the history of the colony." Asher said.

"Oh, good," Abel said. "I have a program I want to test at the library." Abel goes to his drawer and pulls out a white T-shirt that contrasts with his darker skin tone. Various anime characters were on the old t-shirt. As he put the shirt on, it scratched his black, wool-like hair. The words ".hack//Sign" were located at the top.

"Maybe I'll find some info out about what's in the sky," Eli said.

"Huh," Asher responded. "Something in the sky?"

"Yeah. I can see it with my telescope. It's like an isosceles triangle. Some odd, cone-shaped object."

"Probably just an asteroid," Asher responded. "I remember something about the original colony disrupting the atmosphere when they got here."

Eli shrugs and reaches into a drawer. He pulled out a black t-shirt that contrasts with his pale skin. A cartoonish character with brown fur and a long nose was on the front, giving a thumbs-up. The word "ALF" was above the image.

"Let's hurry up," Asher said. "I'm not missing supper for this research."

"Right behind you," Abel said, while putting a small thumb-sized device in his pocket.

*****

The Main Kaeldaria library was one of the larger buildings in the town. Any citizen of Kaeldaria could access the information either at home on their pads or come to the unmanned location for a deeper dive into the archives. At 3 stories, it houses all the historical references Asher, Eli, and Abel could need. Located downtown, the 2nd floor has multiple listening stations. Each station is called a dome, and several domes are in each case. If you have a group case, you can listen to and watch whatever someone in your case has.

There are 2 entrances to the library on the North and South sides of the building. Inside, there are wide wooden steps that go to the 2nd floor on the East and West sides of the building. The wooden steps from the 2nd to the 3rd floor are on the North and South sides of the building.

Asher started to get restless in his dome. He waved his hands on the opaque screen of the dome. A lot of this information he already knew.

"...would be the 37th colonizing mission sponsored by the Kael-Daria Corporation..."

"...housing over 50,000 gametes would ensure that there would be plenty of genetic diversity for years..."

"...without the cryo-sleep section of the ship, the crew of 100 scientists, doctors, engineers, and the like, would not live long enough to reach their destination..."

"...should arrive every 30 years. Then we will be able to exchange information with our distant relatives in space. Chet, what would you like to know about the expedition to this 'New Eden'...?"

"See?" Eli said through the mic in his dome. "There are ships that are supposed to come every 30 years. Maybe what I'm seeing in space is a ship from Earth."

"When was the last time a ship came from Earth?" Asher asked. "And why would they hide that news from the colony? Wouldn't it be good news to know we are still in contact with Earth? Wait, didn't you say what you saw in space was cone-shaped?"

"Yeah," Eli responded. "Maybe the tech changed on Earth, and cone-shaped ships are better."

"Maybe..." Asher muttered under his breath.

"I got some other stuff over here you might want to check out," Eli said.

Asher taps the AUX2 button to see what else Eli was watching.

"...expedition did not return at the designated time. The Office of Admin Affairs offers this statement: "Unfortunately, our ability to expand into the woods is impeded by unknown dangers. We are looking into what those dangers are, if they would affect the colony in any way..."

"Hey Eli," Asher says through the mic in the case.

"Yeah, Ash?"

"What year is this broadcast?"

"Um, let me check..." Asher can hear Eli swiping on the inside of his case.

"Looks like 2348 Earthside."

"Were there any other expeditions before this one?"

"Doesn't look like it. This looks like the 1st one."

"An expedition into the woods with only three people?"

"Yeah. And three older people at that. What are they supposed to do in the woods?"

"Huh? Rewind it. Let me see them."

"Ok... See, right here? The cross-reference came up on the screen when the broadcast showed their faces. The reference says they're all around 75 yrs old. It doesn't make sense."

"Nope. It does not."

"Hey, Ash?"

"Yeah, Abel?"

"You guys are going to want to listen to these audio recordings."

Asher taps on the screen and connects with Abel as well.

The audio starts playing:

"Did they make it, Sammy? Sammy, answer me! "

"It was struggling not to go into the vault. Johnson and Hinkley -"

The recording was interrupted by a long pause of static.

...ZZZZTTTT...

"- to do with the demon?! What if'n it breaks free?"

"How are we going to kill it? That's what I want to know. Too many have sacrificed their lives. I want payback in BLOOD!" Multiple voices create a cacophony of confusion on the recording.

BANG! BANG! BANG!

"What's that banging sound?" Eli asked.

"Probably a gavel. Maybe this is in a courtroom or something."

"Gentlemen, I understand that our loss is-"

...ZZZZTTTT...

"-truth is that our weapons had zero effect on the creature."

"That is a DEMON FROM HELL! WE HAVE TO KILL IT!"

"It took my only son! My boy!"

BANG!

"Gentlemen, please! Let's hear from Dr. Killian. He says he has data that could help end this."

"These are my observations, gentlemen. In the last 3 days of hunting and fighting the creature, the only time -"

...ZZZZTTTT...

"The perimeter drones' scans show a wide variation in its energy levels, followed by either an increase or decrease in strength, speed, and/or stamina. When the Volunteer Fire Brigade -"

...ZZZZTTTT...

"...creature immediately dropped, and it stopped moving. Unfortunately, all members of the brigade were lost.

...ZZZZTTTTT...

As the recording ended, a silence hung in the air for a moment.

"Ash?"

"Yeah, Eli?"

"...Are monsters real?"

*****

"Wow. Gen was right." Morgan rolls her eyes. "You're all out of your minds."

Morgan walks into the living room from the kitchen. Even though she was in her early twenties, passing the competency test allowed her to live on her own without being in a college dorm. She gives Trustin and Amelia both a glass of water while they sit on the couch.

"There's no way that will work. You don't have the security clearance even to get close to the main building. And to get to that building, you need clearance for the 1st building. And if you aren't scheduled to work or have a meeting, that might trigger a security breach. And if you have a security breach on your record, that could affect future job prospects. You guys haven't thought this through at all."

"We just want answers," Amelia replies. Someone, somewhere has answers."

"Surely there's some information that can help us understand why so many die in the West Woods," Trustin chimed in. "Have you ever thought about it?"

"Yeah, I have," Morgan said. "But that's how it's always been. They knew a couple of hundred years ago that starting a colony on this planet was dangerous. We're lucky we even exist right now. Think about how many people died *before* this town existed. Those sacrifices enabled the expansion we see today. We have clean water, mining for minerals, and no animals intruding from the woods. Whatever is going on must be working."

"Just because it *looks* like it's working, doesn't make it ok!" Amelia said while gritting her teeth. "You think losing our parents and grandparents randomly makes it ok? If they made things better in the past, why are we still doing this??"

"Ok, that's a fair question," Morgan said in a calm tone. "Let's start with the info you got from people in the town."

"I went to see Ms. Wainwright," Trustin said. "Her husband was on the expedition my granddad and Mr. Butler were on. She kinda seemed too calm to have just lost her husband. I would've expected the subject to trigger some kind of emotion, but she gave me nothing in that regard. She mentioned that they were all in the same graduating class, and when the message came through the signal, Mr. Wainwright said it was his duty to support the expedition into the woods."

"Anything else?" Morgan asked.

"She did make a comment about 'when everyone's turn comes' and 'when was the last time someone had a natural death'. I thought the phrasing was kinda weird."

"What do you mean?"

"It sounded like she was saying that the town was killing people instead of people having natural, full lives. Like the town was in on 'the gag' to some extent."

"Now that you mention it, when *was* the last natural death?" Morgan asked while staring at the ceiling. She leaned back in her chair, and a silence hung in the room.

Just then, Genessa came from one of the bedrooms. The sisters' similar appearance was striking. The long, straight hair, dusky skin, and dark brown eyes were identical. If Morgan weren't a little bit taller and rounder in the face, they could almost pass as twins. In the silence of the conversation, Genessa walked to the couch to sit next to Amelia. Amelia scooted over, closer to Trustin.

"Sorry I yelled at you guys," Genessa said while brushing her hair behind her ear. "The thought of breaking into the woods started to freak me out."

"It's fine," Amelia said while she hugged her friend.

"I just didn't want to see anyone get in trouble or hurt. Even Mr. Number Two over there."

"Excuse me?!" Trustin said, leaning past Amelia and giving Genessa a look. Genessa responded by sticking her tongue out at him.

"Anyhoo..." Amelia said to break the tension. "I did talk to Ms. Wells and Mr. Maclachlan."

"Oh, what happened?" Morgan asked, getting the group back on track.

"Ms. Wells made a point about answering the call and that if my dad didn't go, someone else would, and how I would feel about that option," Amelia said. "She also said that we live in dangerous times and the expedition is needed to learn more about the planet. And she suggested that I speak with Mr. Maclachlan, which I had already planned to do."

"Anything come of talking to Mr. Maclachlan?"

"Maybe," Amelia said. "When I walked in, I noticed his signal bar had a purple light on it, but it wasn't on when I was there. The green light was on. We talked about my dad and how they got along. My ma just told me yesterday that my dad used to be the spokesperson for the Tech Borough."

"Oh wow," Genessa said. "That's my dad's job now."

"It's a long story," Amelia continued. "A couple of things were kinda weird, though. When I got there, he offered me tea. I said no. Then, while we were talking, he rubbed the rim of his teacup, and it made a slight humming sound. Then he asked me again if I wanted some tea. I said no again. So then he said I need to talk to the spokesperson for the outer boroughs to see what their security protocol is for their expansion, but the Security Borough guards the West Woods."

"Oh, brother," Trustin interrupted. "Sounds like he's blowing you off."

"Exactly," Amelia agreed. "In anticipation of getting blown off, we decided to meet up over here. Two things I'm noticing when interviewing people. One: Everyone I talked to kept kicking the can down the road. Two: Only certain people have a purple light in their house. Everyone doesn't have it."

"You have one, Morgan," Trustin said, nodding toward her signal bar.

Morgan looked at her signal bar in the living room and stared at the green light, which was on, and the purple light, which was off.

"I don't think the purple light comes on a lot. That bar was installed when I got the job a couple of weeks ago. The installation crew tested it while I was here. The purple light gave me a really bad migraine."

"Funny you said that," Amelia said while showing Morgan the bracer on her left wrist. "The first time I put this bracer on, a purple light came out of it and gave me a migraine, too. I got it from my mom the other day. She said it was a gift from her new job."

"Ok, listen up," Morgan said while putting her elbows on her knees. If something strange or dangerous is going on in town, try to keep quiet about it. If you make too much of a stink, you might get labeled, and that could cause other issues."

"Labeled? What label?" Amelia asks. Morgan took a deep breath before she continued.

"Everyone in town has a file. Those files contain everything you've ever done in the town, for the town; build something, dog walking, you name it. If you are someone known for 'disturbing the peace' or 'town drunk', you get a label in your file. Some of these labels come off your record, some don't."

"Wait, you've seen these files?" Trustin asks in an inquisitive tone.

"No, I haven't *seen* them per se, but I know they exist."

"Interesting..." Trustin stands up and starts a slow pace around the room. "Depending on the labels, that could change job prospects, schooling, housing, etc. The labels that don't come off, when would they get them, and how many labels that don't come off could someone have? If someone has behavioral issues, if they have genes with a higher rate of cancer or heart disease. Would they be willing to cull the populace for a 'better tomorrow?' Depending on the labels, the government may be sending people into the woods to get rid of troublemakers, instead of letting the tribunal decide the punishment for the crimes."

"OK... that sounds barbaric." Morgan trails off in a quiet tone. "I understand what you're saying, but I don't like where this train of thought is taking us. Are you automatically assuming that the government is doing something bad or wrong just because you are personally affected?"

"We don't have to be affected for it to be wrong," Amelia responded.

"And people are dying with zero consequences," Trustin said.

"Something is going on with these purple lights and the expeditions, sis," Genessa commented. "You gotta see that. Somehow it's all connected. It's starting to sound like the lottery really is rigged, and that random people aren't selected to go to the woods. And for some reason, there aren't any protests or any talks about it in the news. Isn't this a big deal that should be discussed?"

DINGDING! DINGDING!

The bell rang for Morgan's apartment.

"That's Asher, I'm sure," Trustin said.

Morgan looked at her own bracer and tapped a button, letting Asher in the building.

"I wonder what he found at the library," Amelia said

"I forgot proxies don't have bracers. Otherwise, he could have just sent us the info."

The apartment door opened, and Asher came in. He looked like he had seen a ghost.

"You ok, Ash?" Genessa asked.

"You guys, we have to get to the library!" Asher said as his hands trembled.

"What did you find out?" Morgan asked.

"We, uh, we heard some audio recordings from back in the day. It sounded like there was a monster in the woods. I'm not sure if they captured it or what's going on. I-I don't know what we got into by looking this stuff up. Maybe there's a reason the townsfolk don't bring up the woods. Maybe they know. Maybe they *all* know what's in the West Woods!" Asher said, exasperated.

"How did you get to those particular files?" Amelia asked.

"Abel had some hack program and something he said with the root directory. I don't know all that technical stuff. Whatever he did, he found an audio file I don't think we were supposed to hear."

"Where are the twins now?" Morgan asked.

"I told them to go home. They don't have bracers, and Abel wasn't able to save info on the chip that he brought with his hack program on it."

"Ok, guys," Morgan said with an even keel. "This is what you do: Go to the library and find those files."

"We won't have access without Abel. He had the chip that hacked the thing."

"Ok, I'll call Tron House and have the twins meet you back at the library. When you get the info, save it to your bracers and bring it back here. Call your parents and make up an excuse for why you aren't home yet. I have to be at work in 30 minutes. My shift is just a few hours since I'm new. I'll try to find out what I can on my end and see you when I get back. Be careful. Don't draw attention to yourself, ok?"

The four of them nod in agreement. Morgan hugs her sister, and the group heads toward the library.

Chapter 4

In the Spokesperson's mansion on the North Side of Kaeldaria, Ira Edward heads toward his office. Inside the office, he walks over to the mahogany desk, gifted to Trustin by Ira's Father-In-Law. He pushed a button underneath the desk, and the bookcase behind him moved into a recess in the wall. It slid to the side, and he walked into a small, dark room. The bookcase slid back into place behind him.

The room was the size of a very small closet. No room to sit; just a touchpad and a view screen. He tapped on the touchpad, and the viewscreen came to life. One by one, floating heads appeared on the viewscreen. Their visage blackened out. A box appeared on the screen that said, "Voice identity required."

"Meat Packing Borough.
Delta-Five-Three-Eight-Epsilon. Confirm."

"Confirmed," the computer voice said back.

"The Council brings this meeting to order," a mild voice said.

"What is this urgent matter, Tim?" Ira asked.

"The Butler child is no longer controlled," Tim said.

"How do you know for certain?" one of the darkened heads asked.

"I performed the ritual, and she did not respond," Tim replied.

"What were you discussing with the child? Why was she talking to you?" a voice asked.

"She said she had a history project due and was asking about the West Woods. I performed the triggers during the conversation, but she failed all of them. So I deemed her broken and called for an emergency counsel session."

"Is there a reason for her breaking?" Another darkened head asked. "Is something out of the ordinary happening with the child?"

"She and her mother are in the process of moving to the admin building per the agreement struck with her father," one voice replied. "Possibly the stress of the move has temporarily created the break."

"That has happened in the past. Once the move is complete, the daughter will again be subjected to the suggestions from the signal bars at home and at school. She will be under control soon enough." A darkened head said.

"I disagree," Ira said.

"Why is that, Ira?"

"My son came to me yesterday asking about an expedition to the West Woods. I believe he may be involved with this. This isn't his first time asking about it, and I don't think it will be his last." Ira said.

"Because he is the child of a Spokesperson and lives at home, he is not under the suggestions. Do you think he should be subjected to them?" A voice asked.

"I do," Ira responded. "His relationship with his grandfather was very strong. Losing him had a worse effect on Trustin than I anticipated. With his mother and grandfather gone, our relationship is forced to become something that neither one of us wanted. I will not jeopardize my station because my child is unruly. His food and the water are already medicated. All that is left is to install the proper signal bar in the home, and he will fall in line within a matter of days. I need a co-sign from the counsel to implement this plan."

"The textile borough co-signs," Tim said.

"The mining borough co-signs," another voice said.

"Then it is agreed," Ira responded. "I will contact -"

BEEPBEEP! BEEPBEEP! BEEPBEEP!

An alarm sounds from the computer, and the viewscreen displays a red, flashing dot.

"Unauthorized access from the Main Kaeldaria Library."

"WHAT?!" a voice shouted.

"How is this possible?" another voice shouted.

"People, please. Lets keep our wits, shall we?" a mild voice said. "Computer, what was accessed?"

"Information regarding the colony ships, various expositions, and damaged recordings," the computer answered.

"Computer, move the accessed information into a temporary classified subdirectory. Please give it 512-bit encryption and send the access information to my terminal. I'll address it later and let everyone know what I find," the mild voice said.

"Processing... command completed," the computer voice said.

"Good," the mild voice said. "Occasionally, someone gets curious, and we shuffle the files around. The suggestions kick in, and the individual forgets about it in time. Nothing to worry about. If there is another attempt to access the information, we can have the security team apprehend the individuals. So where were we?"

"I will get the installers to bring in a new signal bar for the living room. If there are any other disturbances, let's keep each other apprised, agreed?" Ira asked.

The voices agreed.

"Meeting adjourned," Tim said.

The viewscreen went dark, and Ira turned off the computer.

*****

The Main Kaeldaria Library's doors slid open as Amelia and her friends entered. Eli waved at the group from the 2nd-floor glass balustrade. Asher waved back, and they started heading toward the stairs. As soon as Amelia crossed the building's threshold, her bracer made a curious sound.

BEEP

“What was that?” Trustin asked.

“What was what?” Amelia responded.

“I heard a beep from your direction. Was that your bracer?”

“I wasn’t paying attention,” Amelia said as they walked to the stairs for the second floor.

BEEP

“Ok,” Genessa said. “I heard it that time. That’s your bracer, Amelia.”

The group paused by a bookshelf, and Amelia lifted her left arm. As the group paused to look at her bracer, a purple light shone from the small viewpad.

“AAHHHH!” Asher yelled.

“My eyes!” Genessa screamed out.

A few people in the distance looked over in that direction, distracted from their own research.

“It’s fine. Everyone’s fine,” Trustin said, reassuring the gawkers.

Eli came downstairs to check on his brother.

Amelia and Trustin guided Genessa and Asher to a reading spot on the 1st floor with some comfortable chairs.

"That's what happened to me when the purple light hit me in the eyes," Amelia said. "You guys stay here. It'll only last a few minutes. I'll head toward the listening stations with Trustin and see if Abel can get access to the info from earlier. Eli, stay with them, we shouldn't be long." The three of them nodded in agreement as Amelia and Trustin headed to the 2nd floor.

Amelia and Trustin saw Abel at the listening station. As they headed toward the listening station, Abel stood up and emerged from the case. With redness in his eyes, he wipes his face with his hands.

"What happened, Abel?" Amelia asked.

"It's gone. All of it is gone." Abel said with strained words.

"What do you mean? What's gone?" Trustin asked.

"All the information we saw about the colony and the monster is gone. We don't have a way to prove that something is being hidden from the town. We don't have any way to prove there is or was a monster. And no one is going to believe us because we're proxy kids."

"We believe you, Abel. We always believed you guys," Amelia said as she put her hands on Abel's shoulders.

BEEPBEEP

A chime comes from Amelia's bracer.

"We will ignore that for now," Amelia said.

"Show us what you did before," Trustin said.

They walked over, and Abel sat in the pilot's chair for the station. The viewscreen comes from behind the chair and goes above and over Abel's head until it rests at a comfortable distance in front of him. A touchpad keyboard slid from behind the screen and in front of Abel. He started tapping on the keyboard and sent a command that opened a port on the chair he's sitting in. He reaches into his pocket and pulls out a small rectangular device that fits into the port.

"So last time I searched in the directory," Abel said, "I came to these folders and used my drill program to get into the root directory, no problem. But now when I try to do it, this happens..."

The screen turns crimson.

"That doesn't look good," Trustin said.

"It didn't do this last time," Abel said. "Last time, it gave a list of folders, each labeled with a time period on Earth. Now there's nothing."

"The lack of evidence is still evidence," Trustin said. "Somehow, someone knows you shouldn't have seen that info, and they deleted it or moved it. I think this red screen triggered an alarm."

BEEPBEEP

"Oh no!" Abel exclaimed. "I don't want to get in trouble! I just wanted to see what else was on the servers!" Abel said, exasperated. "It feels like we proxy kids are always in the dark about everything. I just wanted... it doesn't matter." His voice trails off as he lowers his head. He pushes a button and disconnects the chip from the port, and the viewscreen goes back behind the pilot's chair. As he stood up, Amelia reached out and hugged him.

"Abel, you matter," Amelia said. "What you want and need matters. We will all get answers together, ok?"

Abel backs up and nods while wiping his eyes.

"You mentioned servers. If we can't get the info from the domes, can we get the info from the servers directly?" Trustin asked.

"We should. In theory," Abel said. "If the info has been deleted, that's a different problem than if it's been moved. We would need a recovery program to undelete the info, if that's even possible..."

Trustin attempted to say something, but Amelia touched his arm and shook her head. She knows Abel needs to talk this out. There was a time to speak. But this was a time to listen.

"If the info has been moved, we might be able to find where it's been moved to," Abel said. "If there are multiple servers, we could look in the history and track where it went. But even if we find it, it'll probably be encrypted again. Maybe with stronger encryption. And I don't think my program will be able to open it then." Abel had a slight frown on his face.

"Well," Trustin said. "Let's solve one problem at a time. For starters, where are the servers?"

"Oh yeah," Abel said. He put his hands on his sides, looked around, and mumbled, "If I were a server, where would I be...?" He wandered away from the domes in the listening station and walked around the library.

"Well, they wouldn't be on the 2nd floor. That wouldn't make any sense. For a building this size, they should probably be on the 3rd floor or the 1st floor."

Amelia pulled up her bracer and tapped it a couple of times.

"How you guys doing down there?" she asked.

"We're ok," Genessa responded. "All the headaches are gone. We were just about to come to you."

BEEPBEEP

"Instead of doing that," Amelia said, "Do us a favor: Abel says we should be looking for where they keep the servers. The info we need is on them. He said they are either on the 1st floor or the 3rd floor. We're headed to the 3rd floor. Can you guys look for them down there?"

"That's fine," Genessa said. "I don't think I know what servers look like, though."

"Hi Genessa! This is Abel," Abel said as he spoke into the bracer. "You're looking for rectangular-shaped boxes. They don't look like the viewscreens we have in our homes at all. They produce heat and need to be cooled. See if there's a locked room. Or if there's a door that's really cool to the touch."

"Ok. Got it. We will let you know if we find anything." Genessa said.

"Us too. See you soon," Amelia replied.

Amelia, Trustin, and Abel head toward the next flight of stairs to go to the 3rd floor. Meanwhile, Genessa, Asher, and Eli start their search on the 1st floor.

The 3rd floor had a glass balustrade that allowed you to see through the middle of the building. It also had a denser collection of books. Amelia noticed that these books seemed thicker than the books on the other floors.

"Most people are on the 1st and 2nd floors," Trustin said. "Let's split up and meet back by the stairs in a few minutes." Amelia and Abel nod and go their separate ways.

*****

As the afternoon became evening, a small gathering was held at a spokesperson's mansion. The colonial-style home featured a white exterior with cool grey accents. Inside, various guests in proper attire engaged in discussions about art, music, fashion, history, and the like. Among the crowd was Tim Maclachlan and his much older wife, Gloria. Ira Edward was also in appearance, with a young mistress on his arm. The statuesque, almond-toned beauty whispered in Ira's ear and started to mingle with the guests. He had not yet discussed the prospects for marriage with the

Council. Because Trustin would soon succumb to the suggestions, he would no longer be fit to inherit the spokesperson position. A new heir would be needed.

A man of imposing stature came into the gathering area. More than two meters tall, his blonde curls made him one of the tallest gentlemen in the room. Wearing a cool grey pinstripe suit with a white vest underneath and a red tie with a full Windsor knot, he made sure to greet everyone. They were his constituents, after all. He sees his friend Ira in the crowd and heads that way.

"John Robbins! Welcome back!" Ira said while extending his hand.

"Good to be back, my friend," John said in a mild voice as the two performed a Roman handshake.

"I apologize, we had to speak about such serious matters before your welcome back party," Ira said above the cacophony of voices.

"No, no. It's fine. I would rather we handle matters quickly than have them snowball out of control. It all worked out." John said while gesturing toward the kitchen.

"How was your nap? Restful, I hope?" Ira asked.

"Of course. It was only a year, though. The other spokespeople always pitch in when one of us takes a little nap. It's not like I woke up to a pandemic or civil war." John said with a mild chuckle. "Who's next in line?"

"Janet is. That's why she's not here." Ira said.

"Oh, she's down there already?" John said. "She didn't waste any time. The expedition isn't for a few days."

"Can you blame her? Her husband is useless because of his... 'thing'. So we had to put him under the 'heavy' suggestions while you were out. Timber production is down 20% in her borough due to slow population growth. And her kids are a nightmare. She could use the break."

The two men entered the kitchen and walked over to the bar.

"Good day, gentlemen. Your drink orders?" The bartender asked.

"An old-fashioned, Mr. Tron. Thank you." John said.

"And you, sir?" the bartender asked.

"A martini with 2 olives. Make it dirty." Ira responded.

"Right away, sirs," the bartender stated.

"Sorry about the business with Trustin, old friend," John said. "Looks like you have things handled, though. Giselle, eh?" John asked while raising a slight eyebrow. "You always liked brunettes."

"You know me too well," Ira chuckled. "The expansion is progressing on the Northside of my borough. My security team has procured twenty-two more acres. The engineers are getting the fences installed as we speak. The area will be secured and annexed into the Meat Packing district within the next three days."

The bartender places the drinks on the bar. Ira raises his glass.

"Sweet dreams, Janet," Ira said.

The two men toast and start walking toward the veranda outside the kitchen.

"Excellent." John commended. "I've never doubted your expansion efforts. I wish some of the other spokespeople and security teams were as efficient as you and yours. The birth rate has slowed significantly over the last couple of years. But that's to be expected because of the suggestions. Were there any candidates that stood out to the spokespersons for the new borough?"

"It wasn't even mentioned in the borough meetings while you were sleeping," Ira said. "The spokespeople as a whole lack ambition."

The two men head outside towards the west veranda. The sun was still above the tree line. The sky was changing into vibrant shades of red, purple, and orange.

"We knew they would grow soft. That's why the outer boroughs created the Council. To keep this colony growing and expanding. We can't afford to get soft or sloppy. Especially since assistance from Earth stopped decades ago."

"Or more specifically, we stopped it," Ira stated. "We may need to rethink assistance from Earth if we want the expansion efforts to increase."

"I thought the same, old friend," John said. The issue is that anything that comes from Earth will bear Earth's logic. An Earther's way of speaking, thinking, ruling. And we have no idea how they would react to the little experiment we're running 'in the basement'. I'm sure that wouldn't go over well. We'd have zero say in stopping any social, economic, or military force they would bring with them. Our way of life would be wiped out, and nothing we've built here would have ever mattered."

"Then we need to rethink how to use the sleep capsules to our advantage," Ira said. "If we can't expand as rapidly as we would like, then the council needs more time to get the colony to where we want it to be."

"Agreed. I won't be able to use the capsule for another five years. We need to reconvene the council and reschedule –"

BEEP BEEP BEEP

BEEP BEEP BEEP

John pushes back his left sleeve and sees a red light on his bracer. He locked eyes with Ira and tapped on the bracer.

"Report," John said in a mild voice.

"Another hack has been attempted at the Main Kaeldaria Library," a computer voice said.

"Dispatch a fire team to the library and convene the council. Have the culprits interrogated at the nearest detention facility."

"Instructions confirmed." The computer voice said.

"This annoyance is becoming a nuisance," Ira said with an agitated tone.

"We will see how far this goes, my friend," John said with a mild voice.

Chapter 5

At the Main Kaeldaria Library, a message goes through the building:

"Attention, citizens. The Library will close in 15 minutes for maintenance. We apologize for the inconvenience. Thank you and see you soon."

"You guys find anything?" Genessa asked Asher and Eli. "Sounds like we have to leave soon."

"Since when does the library close?" Asher responded. "It's not even a manned building."

"Yeah," Eli chimed in. "We're here all the time. That's weird. But this room over here looks interesting."

The three of them walk over to the room. The room is at the back of the library, against the west wall. There's a cool draft coming from the slight crack underneath the door. The door doesn't have a handle, and there is a pad on the right side.

"Did you guys find anything?" Genessa said into her bracer. "We got something that looks promising."

"No," Amelia said. "We can come to you. Where are you?"

"The west end of the library," Genessa said. "There's a door on the west wall."

"The west wall?" Amelia asked. "I wonder if that's a coincidence. See you in a few minutes."

"Where are you?" Genessa asked. "Is your bracer still beeping?"

"On occasion. I don't know what's wrong with it. It was beeping more on the 2nd floor than on the 3rd."

"Was it beeping before, or is this a new thing? Like, did it beep when you 1st got it? Does your mom know it beeps?"

"It just started when we came into the library."

"Huh. I wonder if it will beep more when you get to this room. Maybe it's trying to tell you something."

"Well, we're about to find out."

As Amelia, Trustin, and Abel head toward the north side stairs, Trustin, from the 3rd-floor balustrade, sees an armed security team enter the building from the South. The young-looking men were wearing wine-colored uniforms with gold piping. 2 team members guarded the door, and 2 began questioning the citizens leaving the library.

"Wait. Let's see how this plays out," Trustin said.

The 3rd-floor trio watches as the officers go to the 2nd floor and start asking around. The officers walk toward the listening station, out of sight. Amelia sees Abel shaking and puts her hand on his shoulder.

"It'll be alright," she said.

"Let's make our way to the 1st floor," Trustin said.

"Hey, guys," Amelia said to her bracer. "We might have an issue. We think there's a security team at the listening station. I think they're looking for us."

"Yeah, we see them," Genessa said. "You're so close to figuring this thing out, Amelia! What should we do?"

"You guys stay out of sight," Trustin interrupted. "We'll come to you." Trustin looked at Amelia and asked, "With your mom's new job and the move to the admin building, do you think that bracer is part of this? If it is, and they catch us, they are probably going to take it for evidence."

"I hadn't thought of that," Amelia said. "We need to stay out of the officers' line of sight. Let's stay closer to the wall, away from the middle. We can't see them, but they can't see us either."

Trustin and Abel nod in agreement. The three of them make their way to the other side of the bookshelves, opposite the balustrade, and start walking the long way around the west wall to the north steps.

BEEP

"What was that?" One of the officers asked his partner.

"Seriously?!" Trustin whispers to Amelia. "Now it decides to beep?"

"Sounds like it came from the 3rd floor. Let's check it out," the other officer said.

"Look where we are," Amelia whispers in response. "We are 2 stories above the server room. The beeping has to mean something."

"For now, let'd dodge these officers," Trustin said. "If the beeping increases the closer we get to the server room, we don't want to go there while they are looking for us." The group headed toward the north wall on the 3rd floor and crouched down behind some bookcases.

The officers head upstairs toward the west wall, where they heard the noise.

"Dispatch, this is Unit XO-1," He said into his bracer. "We disconnected the listening stations as instructed. We were able to interview a few people about the stations. They said there were 2 boys and a girl around the station that aligned with the timing of the alarm. The library is empty now. They must have left before we got here. Any further instructions?"

"No," said a familiar voice.

Amelia and Trustin smile at each other.

"The disconnection of the domes is fine for now. We have more passive ways to deal with the situation that will keep it under wraps."

"Understood," the officer said. "Also, there was a beep sound coming from the 3rd floor. Any idea what could cause that? I'm not familiar with any electronics on the 3rd floor of the library."

"From the inside or the outside of the building?" A familiar voice asked.

"Uh, that's unclear, dispatch. Everything looks normal on the inside." The officer said.

"Good job," The familiar voice said. "Check the perimeter and return to base for debriefing."

"Roger that," The officer responded. The 2 officers head downstairs and outside. Once outside, the 4 officers head toward the parking lot and out of sight of the entrance.

The trio on the 3rd floor headed toward the 1st floor.

BEEP

"I always liked Morgan," Trustin said. "She was the coolest babysitter we ever had by far."

"Oh, please," Amelia said. "You've had a crush on Morgan for years."

"Whaaa!" Trustin stammered. "I don't know what you're talking about. I remember times when kids would try to get me in trouble, and Morgan would speak up. Whenever I played at Tron House, Ms. Tron never spoke up if something was amiss. She would just let things happen."

"It's a little better now," Abel spoke up. "The bigger kids take care of us, sort of. We aren't bullied as much."

"In Tron house or outside of Tron house?" Trustin asked.

"Both," Abel replied.

A wave of sadness washed over Trustin and Amelia's faces.

"Sorry to hear that," Trustin said. "We will have to do something about that when this situation is over, yeah?"

Abel smiles and nods as they reach the 1st floor.

BEEPBEEP

"Oh, God! I thought I was going to die!" Genessa said as she and Amelia hugged. "My heart is beating through my chest! Are you ok?"

"We're fine," Amelia said. "How is everyone?"

"Better now," Asher said while giving a bro handshake to Trustin, while Eli and Abel hugged each other.

"Well, let's see what happens with this door," Amelia said. The group walked over to the door on the west side of the 1st floor. As Amelia comes up to the door, she puts her bracer by the pad. The group heard multiple chirps from her bracer. A progress bar appeared on the pad. When the progress bar finished, the door slid open. A cool breeze wafted from inside. The room was dimly lit and rectangular. It was about 21 meters long. The group had to turn right immediately upon entering the room. The servers were 3 meters tall, 1 meter wide, and 1 meter deep. They were aligned symmetrically against the wall. Blue and green light flickered from the servers' front panels. The group entered, and the door slid closed.

BEEPBEEPBEEP

"Ok, it's trying to tell you something," Genessa said.

Amelia slowly walked to the end of the room.

BEEPBEEPBEEP

The lights on the server at the end of the room stopped. A few seconds later, the server was powered off.

*wwrrrr. CLICK. wwrrrr."

The server at the end of the wall started to recede into the floor. As it went into the floor, handholds were revealed on the North wall at small intervals.

"Look," Amelia said. "We can climb down."

"Hold on, what are we doing?" Trustin asked. "We don't know what's down there. And we have these kids with us. What if we can't get back up?"

"That door already closed behind us, Trustin," Amelia said while grabbing the 1st handhold. "If you were worried, you should have asked that before now. Aside from that, Eli and Abel helped us get this far. They are a part of this now, whether you like it or not. If they leave now and the security forces get them, you think they are going to treat proxy kids nice?"

The group hears a *CLANG* sound as the servier hits the bottom of the opening. Amelia grabbed the handholds and started to climb down.

Just then, a red progress meter appeared on her bracer, showing '60'.

She shows it to the group.

56...

54...

"Hey guys, I think this is a countdown," Amelia said.

"A countdown to what?" Genessa asked.

"I don't know, but red is usually bad," Amelia said as she headed down.

46...

44...

"Speaking of bad," Trustin yelled down to Amelia. "I think this is a bad idea. What happened to getting gear and being prepared?"

40...

"Too late for that. We probably can't go back out the main entrance to the library without setting off some silent alarm. And we don't know what will happen once this server goes back up. What if this is a one-shot deal, like the chip Abel has? How do we know we could even come back if we wanted to? The only way forward is down."

30...

"Well, if I came this far with her, I can go a little farther," Genessa said as she headed down. Abel and Eli head down after her.

Asher shrugs and starts down the handhold. Trustin follows.

24...

"The back of the server has handholds, too," Amelia said. "Be careful, guys."

At the bottom of the climb is a well-lit round tunnel with a round curve. The group can't see the end of the tunnel. The 4-meter-high tunnel had been drilled with machinery that was nowhere in sight. The smooth concrete finish was reinforced at intervals by steel beams that curved around the entire tunnel. The rails in the ground indicate that a tram of some sort was used in this tunnel.

BEEPBEEPBEEP

The server started to rise, and the group watched as it returned flush with the ceiling.

*wwrrrr. CLICK. wwrrrr."

"Abandon all hope, ye who enter here," Trustin said.

"Where is that from?" Asher asked.

"Dante's Inferno," Trustin replied.

"The guy who was talking about the rings of Hell?"

"Yeah. Because that's where we are, or that's where we are going to be. Listen, Amelia's bracer is the only thing that opened all the doors and cracked all the codes. You think that's some coincidence? If this is some elaborate trap, we're screwed. And if she keeps pushing forward, we won't be able to go back."

"We already can't go back," Asher said as he pointed to the now locked server above them.

"Trustin," Amelia said with a calm voice, "We are exactly where we want to be and going in the direction we have wanted to go this entire time, toward answers. And I think this thing on my arm is going to help us get those answers." She pointed at her bracer. "Stay here if you want, but I'm about to find out what happened to my dad, and I'll bring back info to stop these stupid expeditions to the West Woods."

The group followed Amelia as she headed toward the tunnel's end. At the end was a slightly oversized door. When the door opened, the group walked into a modest-sized, seated room.

"Huh," Genessa said. "It's odd that it's, like, so clean in here."

There were no buttons or controls for the tram as the door closed. The group felt the room as it moved in the opposite direction from where they had come. There were 2 windows near the top of the room, but no light shone through them while they were in a tunnel.

"Are we at an angle?" Genessa asked.

"I think we are going down and around this curve," Trustin replied.

The group sat in silence, taking in the gravity of the moment. Amelia took in slow, deep breaths and calmed herself. She had waited a year for this moment, and now, answers were en route. She thought about the last day she saw her father; how calm he looked, even though he knew he would never be back home. Is this what's under the west woods? Did my father take a similar route to his death? She thought about Trustin's comment that the bracer could be leading them into a trap. But if there were a chance that she could stop more fathers and mothers from being separated from their families again, she'd take that risk.

Asher held his arms around his brothers. Abel and Eli rocked back and forth, trying to calm their nerves, while Genessa bit her nails.

Trustin sat with his arms folded, eyes fixed on Amelia's bracer. He anticipated that it would beep, glow, or display another light at any moment to tell them what to do next. He was the spokesperson's son and had no idea this place existed. Am I being kept in the dark on purpose? Was his association affecting his ability to be 'in the know'? Genessa was the daughter of a spokesperson, he thought to himself. Is she thinking about her standing in the town and her future as a possible leader? Does she recognize the sacrifice she might be making, or is she here to drag him into something that throws mud on his name?

After a few moments of silence, light shone through the windows. The group stood on the seats to look out the windows.

"What is that?" Eli said.

The group looked into a huge open cave. The cave was well lit, and the air wasn't stagnant. A spire was in the middle of the cave, about 50 meters from the room they were in. The spire looked to be 10 meters high and 6 meters in circumference. It had multiple wires and cables that protruded from its top.

"Looks like some of the wires and cables go east into the bottom of the town. Maybe that's the main server," Amelia said.

"How do you know where we even are?" Trustin asked with a sarcastic tone.

"Because I've been keeping track in my head," Amelia said. She ignored his tone and focused on the information they had at hand.

"Think about it; The server room was on the west wall. So we were facing west when we entered the room. Then we went under the server room and were facing north. But the tunnel curved toward the west, and we were facing west again when we came into this tram.

Now we should be facing west and descending into the cave beneath the town. I don't know how far down we have gone, though. I don't know if we are exactly under the town anymore, either. We should be somewhere under the security borough, but that's debatable."

"Hmph," Trustin made a vocal sign of disbelief. Asher's eyes enlarged as he looked at Trustin in disbelief.

"Look over there!" Abel said while he looked out the window. "What are those round buildings?"

"That's the colony stations!" Eli said. "Those are the stations from Earth. They should have some information about the town and how things started here."

The colony stations were large, round, and metallic. Roughly 280 square meters and 2 stories high, the colony stations were used to house people, equipment, and animals.

"We're coming up to one of the stations," Amelia said. It looks like five of them in a half-moon formation. See? That 3rd station has a movable corridor that goes to the spire in the middle. So all these stations are connected, and we should be able to reach the middle one.

"How far you guys think we've gone?" Genessa asked.

"Dunno. Feels like a few kilometers or so," Asher said. "If Amelia is right about us going west, I think we are outside the town..."

"Yeah. And under the West Woods," Trustin said. "But I'm more concerned with the lack of guards. If this place is so important, how is it staying secure?"

"Gotta have the right key," Asher said while pointing at Amelia's bracer.

"Yeah, you and Genessa have bracers, but they don't have what's needed to open these doors," Abel said.

"If there are guards, maybe they're in the colony station we are coming up to," Amelia said while taking a deep breath.

"Hey, hey! Look at this!" Eli said with an anxious tone.

The group went to the windows. Across the opposite end of the cave was another tram. It moved toward the first station in the formation. The tram at the opposite end of the cave was farther away from the 1st station. The group knew they would connect with Epsilon before they could connect with the 1st station.

BING!

"Incoming attachment to Epsilon Station," the computer voice said.

"Oh boy," Trustin said. "If we could see them, that means they could see us..."

Chapter 6

The tram started to slow down.

"Ok, gang, what do we do?" Genessa asked as her voice trembled.

"Uh, what do you mean?" Asher said.

"Whoever is in that other tram, saw us for sure," Trustin responded. "These colony stations are large, but if they sprint here, they can get to us in no time. We need to get to the middle station because it has the connection to the spire."

BING

"Welcome to Epsilon Station," a computer voice said over the intercom of the tram.

"No," Amelia said, "I think we need to find somewhere to hide. We've never been in these stations, so we don't know where to go. But we might have time to get out of sight. My bracer has opened doors, so we should be able to hide and let whoever is on the other tram pass us by. They might think we are another group or that there is a glitch."

"You want to risk what we're doing on a glitch or a mistake?" Trustin said with an incredulous tone.

"You want the six of us to go up against people who know these stations and catch us?" Amelia fired back. "We don't know their numbers, and we don't know how to navigate these stations. We can't beat whoever that is in a head-on confrontation, and we don't know how to lock anyone out of the other stations. We need to find a place to hide. That should be easy enough, look at the size of the stations."

"Genessa and I are children of spokespeople," Trustin said. That should be enough to protect us from trouble." The tram came to a gentle stop and began its unlocking procedure.

WRrrrRW...CLICKCLICK...WRrrrRW

"How can you be protected from trouble that shouldn't exist?" Amelia responded. "Trustin, what do you think they're going to do with us if they catch us? This is some super secret government conspiracy stuff. If you were supposed to know about this, your bracer would open all these doors. Whatever is going on with the government, we aren't supposed to be here. Being adjacent to privilege won't get anyone out of this. We need to collect proof and get back to the town."

"I don't think my dad thinks I'm serious enough to tell me any secrets about the town," Genessa said while she looked at the floor. "I guess I hadn't thought about it. We still have a year of school before university. I figured I would worry about that later."

"We need to be pragmatic about our future," Trustin said. "And we don't know how being here, doing this, is affecting that future."

"I can't think about the future while we are going through this," Genessa said, standing up. "Let's get this thing sorted. Then we'll think about that other stuff." She faced the tram's exit door with a determined look. Amelia stood next to her and, for a moment, they held hands.

"You can do what you want, Trustin, but I'm going to try to hide," Amelia said. "I'm not telling anyone what to do. But I didn't come this far to get caught now."

*****

"Welcome to Alpha Station," a computer voice said over the intercom of the tram.

The tram came to a gentle stop and began its unlocking procedure.

WRrrrRW...CLICKCLICK...WRrrrRW

PPSSSHHH

The tram door opened, and four Security Officers with salt-and-pepper hair stepped out. Armed and weapons at the ready, the Navy Blue uniforms with gold piping stood out against the colony station's black-and-white interior.

"Attlee, lockdown that door. Nothing comes in or goes out of the station until we conduct a thorough sweep," said the man with a stern voice.

"Yes, Major," Attlee said. He steps over to the pad on the right side of the closed door and lifts his sleeve. He reveals a bracer on his left wrist, taps it, and a red light shines from the pad.

KLA-KLUNK! KLA-KLUNK!

The emergency brake system engaged as the other 3 officers began their sweep. Attlee stood guard, facing inside the colony station. The Major waved his left hand, and one of the guards walked down a short corridor and pushed a button. A sizable hexagon-shaped plate descended from the ceiling. As he stood on the clear plate, it lifted him to the 2nd floor for a sweep.

"Clear!" the officer said to the Major as he yelled down to the 1st floor.

When he was done and came down, it returned to its original position in the ceiling.

"Clear!" another voice yelled. The Major told the officers that they were continuing their sweep. They made their way through the connected tunnel to the next colony station. As they exited Alpha Station, the Major signaled for the hatch to be locked. The officer conducted the same procedure Attlee had performed earlier.

KLA-KLUNK! KLA-KLUNK!

The emergency brake system engaged as Alpha Station was officially locked down. The 3 officers continued to Beta Station. The configuration inside was different from Alpha, but the main layout was the same; the Major waved his hand, and they swept and locked the stations until they reached Epsilon. They go to the tram, and their sweep is complete.

"Locking it down, sir? One of the officers asked.

"No, Pitt," the Major replied. "Attlee, come in."

"Attlee here, sir."

"Team, we are going to channel five for comms and using channel three for base. Cromwell, you're on me. Understood?" the Major asked.

"Copy that," Attlee said.

"Copy that," Pitt said.

"Copy that," Cromwell said.

"This is Churchill to command," the Major said. "Our sweep has concluded. We are sending the Alpha and Epsilon trams back for inspection. Officer Pitt will accompany the Epsilon tram, and Attlee will accompany the Alpha tram. The officers will conduct a thorough investigation of all the tram systems and report afterward. Sergeant Cromwell and I will conduct a routine patrol until we conclude that the stations are safe."

"Very well, Major. You may proceed," a voice from his bracer stated.

Attlee and Pitt leave on the trams while the Major and Cromwell start their patrol and head back toward Alpha Station.

When Epsilon Station became empty, Amelia and her friends emerged from the floorboards and other hidden compartments.

"Those voices didn't sound familiar," Trustin said. "I think those officers are different from the ones at the library."

"I think so too," Amelia said. "With those officers around, we don't have much time. We have to get access to the computers and download the info. If the officers stay on the 1st floor, we need to be on the 2nd floor to stay out of their way."

"That doesn't matter if we can't unlock any of the doors," Trustin said. "You're the only one who has been able to unlock the doors, Amelia. We need to split up, but we can't get to the other stations."

"Then let's make sure we can get as much info out of this station 1st," Asher said. We had to hide before we could check it out. It'll be a little while before they come back this way, and we can hear the lock when they are coming inside this station." Everyone agreed and began exploring Epsilon Station. As the group heard the lock, they would hide, then reveal themselves in a life-or-death game of cat-and-mouse.

The workstations were downstairs, but there were personal workstations in the bedrooms upstairs. There were 3 identical bedrooms upstairs on the east wall of the 2nd floor. Next to the bed were drawers and a desk with a workstation. There was a pair of earbuds in each desk drawer. The workstation by the drawers needed passwords that Amelia's bracer unlocked. Abel entered the directory system and found various folders.

"I can't access these folders without turning on the computers downstairs," Abel said. "These comps are just terminals. They don't house any info."

"If we turn on the comps downstairs, will that attract attention?" Eli asked. "Won't the officers know they weren't on before? How long will it even take for these old things to boot up?"

Abel just shrugged.

"I'll get it," Amelia said. "Which one needs to be turned on?"

"Uh, the shortcut said the comp name is Colony Orbiter 3," Abel said.

Amelia gave a thumbs up and seized the opportunity to turn on the comps downstairs when the patrol passed by. When she came back upstairs and into the bedroom with the rest of the group, Abel gave her a thumbs-up.

The group watched Abel move around in the folders like a master. Amelia's bracer would beep or light up for a moment anytime Abel hit a roadblock of encryption.

"How did you learn this?" Genessa asked

"Proxy kids have a lot of free time," Abel said. "I've spent the night in the library before just reading and studying. Several games at the library teach you about operating systems. This OS is called Siyabuntu. I learned about it a year ago, but this is really my 1st time seeing it in action. This isn't the OS for anything in the town, as far as I've seen."

"If this isn't the OS in the town, then what info did you see at the library?" Asher asked.

"I dunno." Abel shrugs. "Maybe some info was moved for easy access. Multiple OSes can access the same files, though... WAIT! Wait a minute!"

"SSHHHH!" Eli said, with a finger to his lips.

"What?! What's going on?" Asher asked.

Abel opens a nearby drawer and pulls out a thin, flat cord. He plugs one end into the terminal and the other into a port on Amelia's bracer. A brief download commenced, and then a message on the viewscreen said, "Sync complete". Immediately, five small rectangular boxes appeared on the screen. Each had a name:

- Private Attlee
- Private Pitt
- Sergeant Cromwell
- Major Churchill
- Amelia Butler

"What's going on? What's happening with my bracer?"

"Nothing is happening TO it," Abel said. "Your bracer's OS is Siyabuntu. The comps, appliances, machines, and other bracers all run Chidori OS 4.3. That's why you can open all the doors. It speaks the same language as all these comps and sends out a signal that other bracers wouldn't pick up. The officers have the same OS. That's why they are showing up on this terminal. Look, Trustin and Genessa aren't showing up."

"That doesn't make any sense," Amelia said. "My mom said she got this bracer from work. How would my bracer have Siyabuntu on it if nothing else in town has that OS?"

"Wow, Amelia. Someone your mom knows must've really wanted you to have that," Genessa said. "The timing of you getting that, and like, your mom's job keeps coming up. There's no way it's a coincidence."

"It's not. I think this bracer is my dad's," Amelia said. She felt light-headed and sat on the edge of the bed. All she could do was look at the bracer. Genessa sat next to Amelia and put her arm around her."

"He knew," Amelia said. "He knew I would be here. He knew I would try to figure it out." She closed her eyes and thought of the last time she saw her dad. A torrent of visuals overwhelmed her. Tears streamed down Amelia's face as Genessa hugged her tighter.

Trustin looked at Amelia and felt a tightness in his chest. "*No!*" He thought to himself. 'It is what it is,' His grandfather would say.

"Let's get focused," Trustin whispered to Abel. He let Amelia have her moment. "We need to be looking for info that gives us proof that the lottery is rigged," Trustin said. “And we need to find out what happens on those expeditions to the West Woods. We have circumstantial evidence, but nothing concrete. Let us know when you get to something useful, and we can record it on our bracers.”

Suddenly, Abel stopped moving and just stared at the screen. A folder was on the screen that said “The Proxy Protocol.”

Trustin put his hand on Abel’s shoulder. “Go for it,” he said. Abel opened the folder, and a host of other files and folders were inside. One file was named “Welcome.”

“Here we go,” Trustin said as he passed out one earbud to each of them. Abel waited until everyone was ready, and then he opened the file. A video started playing on the viewscreen. Everyone gathered a little closer to get a decent view.

The video started with a montage of images, and that ended with the slogan “Kael-Daria Inc. A Gift to the Stars.” Then the screen transitioned to a large office and a man sitting behind a nice cherry-oak desk. He has short, straight black hair and tanned skin. He wore the trappings of a scientist. He walked from behind the desk and stood in front of it.

"Hello. My name is Dr. Trafalgar Tron. I am the Lead Scientist and Chief Executive Engineer of the Proximus Protocol, or as we like to call it, "Our Proxy Children." If you are watching this, you have landed safely on your target destination planet. Hopefully, you are thriving, since we meticulously researched the safest planet possible. Epsilon Station, to me, is the most valuable station to come to you."

"This station contains 50,000 zygotes, frozen in suspended animation. Given the dangers of your trip, we could not risk sending large numbers of adults. These zygotes are the future of your entire civilization."

"By now, Alpha through Delta stations have arrived with the proper food and equipment needed to excavate the land and start building strong settlements. However, different planets have unknowables we cannot predict. This is why the proxy children are so special."

"The parents of the proxies are among the best humanity has to offer: scientists, mathematicians, historians, artists, etc. We have chosen those with the lowest rates of disease in their family lines. The proxies are genetically disposed to be cancer and heart disease-free. They are a little more resistant to infections and other airborne diseases, freeing up resources for the original colony members should an outbreak occur."

"The proxies may also surprise you because of their camaraderie and ingenuity. Because the proxies obviously need to be implanted into a uterus, special robots and training will be assigned. As you can tell from your roster, women outnumber men 4-to-1. That would allow for plenty of proxies to be born via surrogacy. None of the proxies is related by blood to the others. This allows for the genetic diversity of your new, expanding colony to be abundant. Without the proxies, genetic diversity would stagnate within 3 generations. As more capsules come, your colony will eventually have the tools needed to travel to other planets from your new home."

"So, in conclusion, join me as we go through 40 lessons to educate you about the specialty station that is Epsilon. By the time you watch this video, sadly, none of us will still be alive. So please, for our sakes, take care of our special children. They are the greatest gift that earth is able to send you."

The video ends and is closed. Abel pushed from the desk and turned to face Eli and Asher.

"We do matter," Abel said.

Chapter 7

"Attlee, Pitt, report," Major Churchill said.

"Area secure, sir," Attlee said.

"Sir, the entrance to the library has been accessed," Pitt said. "Someone was here. There are some faint tracks and footprints on top of the server."

"Good job," Major Churchill said. "Do we know if the perpetrator was coming into the stations or leaving the stations?"

"That part I'm still investigating, sir," Pitt said.

"Understood," Major Churchill said. "I'll order another officer to assist you. Report back when you have additional information."

"Copy that, sir," Pitt said.

"Attlee, confirm that the other trams for stations Beta, Gamma, and Delta have not been used. Then lock those entrances down. That will allow us to start closing in on whoever's involved."

"Copy that, sir," Attlee said.

"Churchill out."

"Sir, are we getting more officers on this?" Sergeant Cromwell asked.

"No," Major Churchill replied. "We want to keep this as contained as possible. The more officers that get involved, the higher the likelihood of an information breach. If there's an information breach, the Spokespeople as a whole will start an investigation into our unit, and that will weaken the Counsel's ability to protect the town from information that could cause a panic."

"Understood, sir," Sergeant Cromwell said.

*****

"That sounded pretty serious," Trustin said while listening to the conversation through Amelia's bracer.

"We have to make a move now to the Gamma station," Amelia said. "With other exits locked off, they are going to close the net on us slowly. Eventually, they will catch us."

"I can stay here," Abel said. "You guys need to turn all the other comps on so I can have more access. That will give me the best way to help from here."

"We can't leave you by yourself," Amelia said. "It's too dangerous."

"I'll stay too," Asher said. "We can at least be a distraction. We can't have the six of us running around, trying to avoid the officers."

"It all goes back to Amelia's bracer," Trustin said. "As long as she's the only one that can do anything, it really doesn't matter who does what; she has to be the one to get everything done."

"Not anymore," Abel said. "We can connect your bracer to the terminal and give you the same OS she has. Then we can duplicate her bracer, and you guys can split up."

"Wait, why do we need to split up?" Genessa asked. "So far, Amelia having the bracer has worked out. It's not making sense to me."

The opportunity to gain the power Amelia has didn't escape Trustin's notice.

"If we do split up," Trustin replied, "We can lock the officers out of Gamma station, find and lock out the other trams, and give ourselves enough time to get to the server in that spire. Abel, can you get more info about that spire? Before he does that, let's make the changes to the bracers so we can get this done faster."

"We don't have enough bracers to go around," Abel said. "We know that this system isn't connected to the town. We need to either connect the stations to the town, open access to the stations, or record the info on the bracers and take it to the town. Something to get this info to the people."

Abel started reconfiguring Genessa's and Trustin's bracer, then replicated the functionality that Amelia's has. Now Amelia, Trustin, and Genessa's bracer are identical to each other.

"So what exactly is the game plan?" Eli asked.

"I think that we need a way to keep the officers trapped so we can do what we need to do," Trustin said. "How can we get them to stay in one place?"

"We'll have to follow them from station to station and jam the locking mechanism," Amelia said. "That's all I can think of."

Abel taps on the keyboard and pulls up some diagrams.

"Ok, look at this," Abel said. "If we get the right comps on, I can network them together. Lock me in the room until everything is over. That way, you won't have to worry about me."

"Not a chance," Asher said.

"Ok, then," Trustin said. "Let's do this; The 3 of us have bracers, yeah? We can split up, and you guys can stay up here and look up the info. As we turn on the comps and you gain more access, you should be able to figure out how to connect the system to the town."

"Ok," Abel said. "If we get a connection to the spire, maybe we can send the info directly to everyone's home through the signal bars and the viewscreens."

"Now we're talking," Trustin said. "Gamma station is probably where everything we want is. We know it connects to the spire. We need to lock the officers into the Alpha station. Is that doable?"

"Yeah. I need to find the controls for the stations," Abel said. "But to lock them in Alpha station, I'll need the comps on in that station. That sounds super risky. And if they turn the comps off and I lose access, they can access another terminal and open the door. Then they will know where we are and how to stop us."

"But you said you'd get us some type of distraction, right?" Amelia said.

"I guess there's something I could do," Abel shrugs. "There's still plenty I need to search through."

"Ok, then," Amelia said. "I'll help trap the officers in Alpha station. They already have the tram locked down. So Genessa and Trustin need to lock down the trams at Beta, Gamma, and Delta stations. Now, how do we keep the trams locked if they have bracers like us?"

"You guys keep talking," Asher said. "Eli and I are going to the other bedroom and connecting to the comps from there. The 3 of us will be able to gather info faster. Abel can run point for whatever shenanigans he's going to cook up. We can hear you through the ear budss." Asher and Eli leave and get set up in the other bedrooms with their respective terminals.

"I guess we're back at the library," Eli said.

"Pretty much," Asher responded.

"So, how are we locking down Alpha station?" Amelia asked.

Abel started looking through different screens and programs. Meanwhile, he connected the terminals that

Asher and Eli were at so the 3 of them could see what each other was doing.

"This should help," Abel said. "This is the Control Interface. It says that, in the event of an emergency, the locks have a double-override feature. It's a redundant failsafe."

Trustin cocked his head and stared at Abel.

"Right, right," Abel said. "Basically, it means that once it's locked, you have to unlock the doors with a bracer and at the terminal at the same time. If you unlock at the terminal, it will relock automatically. Even if they know how to unlock it correctly, it'll buy some time."

"Nice," Amelia said. "I won't be able to keep them from bringing the Alpha station tram down, but I'll be able to lock the tunnel between Alpha and Beta. Then I'll turn on the comps. Trustin can lock the Gamma tram and turn on those comps, and Genessa can get the Delta Tram and then turn on those comps. Then we can meet in Gamma and get to the spire."

"I'll only have access from Beta to Epsilon," Abel said. "But it seems like Gamma is where the most important stuff is."

Trustin and Genessa nod. Genessa hugs Abel from behind while he's seated.

"You guys are so brave!" Genessa said. She kissed him on the top of his head. "Be careful, ok?"

Abel sheepishly nodded.

Amelia, Trustin, and Genessa headed to the hexagon plate and made sure the coast was clear before going to the 1st floor.

"Y'know, it's still, like, oddly clean in here," Genessa said. "For something that's probably a couple of hundred years old, this place is in pretty good shape."

One by one, they head down to the 1st floor.

"I found it!" Abel said. "I found the audio we heard in the library." Abel starts playing the audio:

"Did they make it, Sammy? Sammy, answer me!"

"It was struggling not to go into the vault. Johnson and Hinkley ran at it. Slammed into it and pushed it into the vault. 'CLOSE THE VAULT!' was the last thing we heard Johnson say."

"Aye, bravest lads I've ever had the pleasure of knowing," said the older man

"What are we to do with the demon?! What if'n it breaks free?"

"How are we going to kill it? That's what I want to know. Too many have sacrificed their lives. I want payback in BLOOD!"

BANG!

Amelia and Trustin sprinted for the Gamma station. Genessa locked the tram in the rear of Delta. Then she was able to turn on the comps to the station. She stood on the hexagon plate and went to the 2nd floor.

"Gentlemen, I understand that our loss is great and our sadness very real. However, before we succumb to the subjugation of madness, we must confront the painful truths before us. One of these truths is that our weapons had zero effect on the creature."

"That is a DEMON FROM HELL! WE HAVE TO KILL IT!"

"It took my only son! My boy!"

BANG!

"Gentlemen, please! Let's hear from Dr. Killian. He says he has data that could help end this."

When the officers entered the Alpha station, Amelia sprinted to the door at the opposite end. Trustin was able to lock the tram and turn on the comps in the gamma station.

"These are my observations, gentlemen. In the last 3 days of hunting and fighting the creature, the only time its energy output shifted was when a human made contact with it. The perimeter drones' scans show a wide variation in the creature's energy levels, with some increasing and others decreasing in strength, speed, and/or stamina. When the Volunteer Fire Brigade confronted the creature, they used the fire hose to pressure it against the walls in the alley of Bleeker Street. However, debris on the ground punctured the hose, reducing pressure. The creature took the opportunity to charge through the brigade. When they started wrestling with it and piling on, the creature's energy levels dropped immediately, and it stopped moving. Unfortunately, all members of the brigade were lost.

The recording paused while Abel concentrated on helping.

Amelia ran to the comps and turned them on. She then ran to the door leading to the tunnel for the Alpha station.

"I'm here, Abel!" Amelia said. "We have to get this locked!"

"The comp is still booting up," Abel replied. "I don't have access to that door yet."

"I'm running out of time! What should I do?"

"HEY! IDENTIFY YOURSELF!" Sergeant Cromwell yells from the other side of the tunnel. Amelia runs through Beta Station to the other tunnel. She can hear the officers behind her. The door to the tunnel opens, and she keeps running to the Gamma Station.

"CATCH HER!" Major Churchill said.

BINK!

"ARGH! Sunnva-"

BAP!

Amelia looked back to see the ceiling compartments open, and robots fall out. They were different shapes and sizes, with cleaning equipment attached to their arms. The spinning and whirring caught the 2 officers off guard.

THOOM!

The officers looked up to the 2nd floor as they fought off the small robots.

"What was that?!" The Major said.

THOOM!THOOM!

The hexagonal plate began to lower and revealed a humanoid-shaped robot. It was black-and-white, a mix of metals and ceramics. Its eyes were a lifeless red. When the hex plate landed on the 1st floor, it looked directly into the officers' souls.

"Fallback!" The Major yelled.

They ran back towards Alpha station, and the smaller robots followed. The smaller robots pushed the officers back to the far side of the Alpha station. Amelia ran to the comps and turned them on.

"We see you, kid! We know who you are! Your mother works in the Admin building. You think she's going to keep her position now that we know you're down here?"

Amelia ignored the officers as more small robots swarmed in from the other stations. The robot army nicked and cut the officers on the shins and thighs. The officers started to get overwhelmed.

THOOM!

Amelia looked at the officers and grinned.

"I think you've got company," she said as the hex touched down.

The humanoid robot stepped off the hex and turned toward the officers.

"Permission to open fire, sir?" Sergeant Cromwell asked.

Negative! These robots need to be repaired later to maintain the stations," The Major said.

Amelia exited Alpha Station. She and Abel locked the station, and she ran into Beta Station. She heard the officers swear at the robots and the sound of metal getting smashed.

"You can start the recording, Abel," Amelia said as she locked down the tram and the exit, making her way to Gamma.

"What happened to the Brigade?" a voice in the crowd yells out.

"My uncle was part of that brigade!" another voice yells.

"Well, our analysis shows that the one thing the brigade had that other branch members didn't have was men over 55 years old. We think this creature absorbed energy from them to strengthen itself, and the opposite happened; it was weakened. Our scientific theory is this: the creature is some kind of vampire or parasite that feeds

on our life force or energy. The Fire Brigade's evidence shows that the drain is highly lethal. The Fire Brigade showed that the creature can be poisoned with an older life force. One that is incompatible with its physiology. We have some theories, but I'll turn things back over to the arbiter."

When Amelia got to Gamma Station, Genessa was there to hug her and help her to a seat by the comps.

"Well, Genessa said. "Now we know how this place stayed so clean."

Amelia closed her eyes and took deep breaths.

"Our situation is quite dire," the arbiter states. "The evidence is clear that human energy from someone older than 55 would hurt the monster. However, we don't know how many human lives it would take to subdue or even kill it. It could take hundreds. Maybe thousands." Currently, it may be healing any superficial damage it sustained from the Fire Brigade. We have 3 basic options: Keep it captive until we learn how to kill it. Try to kill it now with volunteers, knowing it's a suicide mission. Or release it and hope it doesn't murder us all. Gentlemen, we need to have a vote on our next course of action."

"That's the whole recording," Abel said.

"So where's the monster?" Amelia asked.

"Did they kill it?" Eli said with a twinge of sadness.

"I-I don't know. Aren't we under the West Woods?" Abel asked, his voice in a high-pitched panic. "Could it still be down here? Has it really killed all the expeditions?" "Not to add salt to the wound, but we have a completely different set of problems now," Trustin said as he came from the back of Gamma Station. "Follow me."

Trustin leads Amelia and Genessa to the back of the station. The trio sees 3 large, capsule-shaped objects in the Med Bay. Trustin walked to a pad on the wall next to the closet capsule. He tapped on his bracer, and a yellow light shone from the pad.

wwwrrrrr

The tops of the capsules moved to reveal their contents. Two were empty. One was not.

"Wait," Genessa said. "That's spokesperson Janet McMurphy. What is she doing in there?"

"Hey, Ash," Abel asked.

"Yeah, Abel," Asher responded.

"You see this on my screen?"

"Yeah."

"What's that word: EL-EYE-SEE-ACH?"

"Lich, Abel. It spells Lich."

Chapter 8

The crunching of metal and ceramic can be heard throughout Alpha Station. Churchill and Cromwell swing at the robots defensively with the butts of their guns. They may not have the strength of young men, but that wasn't going to stop them from doing their duty.

"Code Blue! I repeat, Code Blue!" Sergeant Cromwell yelled into his bracer. After he was done, his bracer went dark. He snatched it off and threw it at one of the robots. It made a whirring sound on impact, adjusted itself, and continued its assault on its 2 victims.

"Code Blue confirmed!" Major Churchill said. "Code Blue confirmed!" He too took off his bracer and threw it at the robots. The two of them held their own until the larger humanoid robots advanced on them.

They pinned the officers against the side door where the tram would enter.

"It's a waiting game now, Major," Cromwell said. The officers heard a slight rumble in the distance.

"Not for long," Churchill said.

*****

"That code blue, the officers just yelled, took all their bracers offline. We can't hear anything from them anymore," Abel said.

"Thanks for the help back there, Abel," Amelia said. You mind looking up these capsules and helping us figure out why a spokesperson is in it?"

"Well, they were stasis capsules for the space voyage," Abel said. "They kept the adults from aging on the long trip."

"Yeah," Trustin said. "I remember that from History class. But what is she doing in it now?"

"I'm trying to find that out," Abel said.

"Hey, guys," Asher said. "Before we go pushing buttons and trying to get to the spire, I think everyone needs to get to a terminal."

"What's going on?" Trustin asked while the trio in the Gamma station went to the comp terminal on the 1st floor of the station.

"There's a lot of info here, and some of these schematics look kind of weird," Asher said. "This one right here is definitely weird."

The group is at the terminal, looking at a schematic titled "The L.I.C.H. Protocols."

The viewscreen showed basic line art and blueprints. The schematic featured a strange humanoid figure.

Height: 2.5 meters.

Weight: 136 kilograms.

Skin Color: Olive Green.

Eyes: Black.

As the schematic moved across the screen, it showed a blueprint of what appeared to be the spire outside the stations. The blueprint showed that the spire was made of various metals to contain the creature. The animation made it clear that the L.I.C.H was in the spire.

"OH, MY GOD!" Genessa gasped when she realized. "It's here!"

"Nobody panic," Trustin said. "It's contained. We're fine."

"I don't think it's that easy, Trustin," Asher said. "The files are saying that the monster has been locked up for over 90 years."

"What?!" Genessa exclaimed. "90 years? Its not dead yet? Why have they kept it for so long?"

Amelia walked over to the round hatch that faced the spire.

"They've kept it captive this entire time?" Amelia said, staring at the spire. "No one in the town is 90 years old. It's been here, locked up, for multiple generations. What does the rest of the file say, Abel?"

"I-I don't wanna say," Abel said as his voice quivered.

"Let me see," Asher said.

Asher tapped the screen and watched an animation. It showed an expedition in a tram with a signal bar. The signal bar had a green light emanating from it. The expedition's posture changed in the animation. Then the expedition entered Gamma Station and walked to the hatch facing the spire. A retractable, covered bridge came from the spire, and the expedition party walked onto the bridge. The bridge then retracted toward the spire. A sequence of doors opened up in the spire that further pushed the expedition team into the spire. One last door opened, and the expedition team disappeared into the spire. Asher covered his mouth as he let out a scream he desperately tried to muffle.

"That's why there are no bodies," Amelia mumbled.

"Huh?" Trustin said. "I'll see what's going on with Asher." Genessa followed Trustin as Amelia stared at the spire.

Silence lingered in the air like a dense fog, hiding the truth. Amelia stared at the spire as Trustin and Genessa came to the same conclusion she did.

"A-Amelia, you need to see this," Genessa stammered.

"I don't need to," Amelia replied. "I know what the spokespeople are doing."

"You sure about that?" Trustin chimed in. "This is looking bad. Sickingly so."

Amelia's chest heaved as she sighed deeply. The sigh of disappointment. Of multiple disappointments.

"The government is feeding the expedition teams to whatever is in the spire," Amelia said. "That's why there are no bodies or any kinds of evidence. And that's why we can't go into the West Woods. We *are* under the West

Woods. The government is using the town above to hide the evidence."

"Our families are part of the government!" Genessa said. "Why would they do this?"

"I don't know why, but I know who does," Amelia said while she pointed at the capsule with Janet McMurphy inside. "We need to wake her up. Any ideas on how?"

"There has to be something here," Trustin said. "As I see it, these capsules shouldn't even be here. These are capsules from Alpha Station. They jury-rigged these capsules here. You think it's got something to do with the spire?"

"I do," Amelia said. "All the other stations were automated to come here, if I remember my history class. These automated stations wouldn't have these capsules. Only Alpha Station would. The bedrooms are for people to work and sleep here after the stations landed. They told us in school that the stations were broken down and used to build the town. They really just built the town on top of the stations. The intention was probably to take the stations apart, but that thing in the spire changed some plans."

"I got something," Abel said from the bedroom.

sshhhhh.... Click. Click. Click. Wwwrrrrr. CLICK. ssshhhhh

The Amelia, Genessa, and Trustin hovered over the capsule's cover. Janet McMurphy's eyes opened. She started blinking, shocked at who she was looking at. The yellow-tinted lid began to move aside, and Janet started to climb out of the capsule. When she got out, the capsule closed and powered down.

"How long was I asleep?" Janey McMurphy asked. "Are you kids spokespersons now? What has happened?" She was in her mid-fifties, of Genessa's height, and somewhat petite. It was clear to anyone seeing her that she was out of breath for some reason and did not stick to the recommended exercise routine. Some grey hair peeked out of her brunette bob. She was wearing a skintight underwater suit and had no jewelry or shoes on. And no bracer.

"Hello, Mrs. McMurphy," Trustin began, using his usual charm with those in power. "We have some questions for you."

"Answer my questions, boy!" She snapped. "I don't care who your father is. If you aren't a spokesperson, you aren't supposed to be down here!"

Trustin, caught off guard by her tone, was rattled.

"We don't know how long you've been down here," Amelia said while she stepped in front of Trustin. "We aren't spokespeople. Our bracers gave us access. We woke you up to ask you about the thing in the spire." Amelia pointed in the direction of the spire.

Janet stomps over to the comp terminal in the room across from the med bay. She started typing and pulled up some information.

"You stupid, stupid children!" Janet said. "Do you know what you've done? This says I wasn't in the capsule for even a full day! Once you start the process, you can't reenter the capsule for another 5 years! And why is this place locked down? Where are the officers? I'll have you arrested for this! Give me your bracer!"

Janet held her hand out to Trustin.

"Hurry up!" She snapped.

A small bead of sweat came from Trustin's hairline. It rolled along the outside of his forehead and hit his eyebrow with a soft touch. Trustin's chest heaved as he inhaled a deep breath. His thoughts were swept up in a whirlwind of emotion. The two seconds Trustin took felt like an eternity. Time slowed to an infinitesimal crawl as he exhaled. He was about to say something he had never said to someone in a position of power.

"No," Trustin said.

Janet backhanded Trustin without hesitation. She reached for his collar to give him another strike.

"NO!" Genessa yelled as she and Amelia grabbed Janet by the arms. The three of them slammed to the floor. Amelia and Genessa held her down. Asher, Abel, and Eli come out of the bedrooms to see what happened. Trustin walks up to Janet and looks down on her. He wipes the trickle of blood from his lip and gives a slight grin.

"I've had worse," Trustin said. "You don't have a way out, and if you want one, you're going to answer our questions."

"I don't have to answer anything, twirp!" Janet barked back. "By now, the officers have called in a Code Blue. Reinforcements will be here soon to carve open these doors and get me out of here."

"Oh really," Trustin said. "That's a shame. Well, we can't hold you forever, and we don't have anything to tie you up with. Why don't we put you back in the capsule?"

"Not that! Anything but that!" Janet shrieked. Amelia and Genessa gave each other a quizzical look.

"Well then," Trustin said. "We are back to asking questions. First off: What's in that spire?"

"An alien," Janet said. "It crashed here almost a century ago. Scientists studied it as best they could and realized the energy it emitted could prolong human life if combined with the stasis fields in the capsule from the Alpha ship. The stasis fields prevent you from aging for long periods. But when combined with the energy from the alien, you could actually heal while in stasis, basically becoming younger. One year in the capsule could reverse 5-7 years of aging."

"But not without a price," Amelia said. "You're feeding the expeditions to that thing."

"Ah," Janet said. "Figured it out, did you? Sorry about your grandfather, Trustin. There wasn't anything we could do. He was already terminal."

"What?" Trustin said. "What do you mean?"

"Your grandfather had cancer, of course. Didn't Ira tell you? That's why he volunteered. He had an aggressive form that couldn't be treated in time. Various diseases affect the human body in terrible ways on this planet. At any rate, this alien was a godsend. The technology on its ship is what allowed the innovations we have."

"Innovations? What ship?" Genessa asked.

"How is keeping that alien locked up a 'godsend'?" Amelia yelled. "How is sending people to their deaths a 'godsend'?" She held even tighter to Janet's arm. Genessa followed suit.

"Those who run this town need to stay alive," Janet. "We give direction so there is no chaos. Those who run this town have the right to the first spoils. Because we have run this town for so long, we know what direction the town should go in. Sacrifices have to be made, but it's for the greater good. We have better meds because of the alien, your bracer, it's his technology. He was wearing it when he got here. We reverse-engineered it and connected it to our older systems. The signal bars give out subliminal suggestions to keep the peace. The

L.I.C.H. Protocols were developed to make sure we can stick around. You won't get away with any of this."

"I'm not worried," Amelia said. "We aren't trying to get away."

"Then what are you trying to do, love?" Janet asked.

"We are going to send the info from the stations to the people in the town," Amelia said.

"Oh, really?" Janet sneered. "And how do you plan on doing that?"

"We are going to connect to the town and send everyone the information to their bracers and viewscreens," Abel said.

"HA!" Janet said with a cackle. "If it were that easy, you would have done it by now. But the devices in the town have a fail-safe. They can't receive information from here. You'd need to record the info on your bracer and then upload it to the servers the town uses."

"You're lying!" Abel said. "We saw this info from the library!"

"Oh, you poor proxy child," Janet said with a tone of condescension. "Look around. How many exits did you lock? Don't you think that the locations where those exits let out would have access to information in here? Of course they would. They would need some access to get down here. You're the one who accessed information in the library, so that tells me you got here from the library."

"Ah, I see," Janet squinted her eyes and relaxed her posture. "Then we locked you out of the system, and you came on this little adventure. Is that it? But now you've locked yourself in here, thinking your little plan would work. So even if you have information on those bracers, you'd have to get past security. And once they get here, you'll all lose your bracers, get brainwashed, and never remember this place. And the signal bars will keep you all nice and docile. And you'll return to your lessons and games, and be happy citizens again. Until we have to feel you to the alien, which I assure you, will be sooner rather than later."

CRAM! CRAM!

ZZZZZzzzzrrrrrrrTTTT

"Ah, my heroes will be here soon," Janet said. Her words had the perfect blend of glee and menace.

The group could hear machinery in the distance. Desperation loomed in the air. Trustin ran across Gamma Station to see what was going on.

"I think they're in the Beta station!" He yelled as he ran back to the group. "I think she's right." Asher looked at Trustin, and they both ran to the back of the Gamma station. The large round hatch to the tram had a tram in front of it. But the lights were off. Trustin and Asher ran back to the group.

"She's right," Asher said. "The trams don't have power. So even if we unlocked the doors, we can't leave. What do we do now?"

"Nothing, child," Janet said. "Sit here and accept your fate," Janet said with weighted finality.

The group stared at each other. They exchanged looks of fear, sadness, and guilt. Little by little, tears started to stream down Abel and Eli's faces. Asher hugged his brothers as Trustin looked at his shoes. Amelia stood up while she held Janet. Genessa and Janet stood as well.

ZZZZZzzzzrrrrrrttt! ZZZZZzzzzrrrrrtttt!

Amelia let go of Janet and stared at her bracer. *He knew I would get this far,* she thought to herself. *I need to talk this out just like he would tell me to.*

"Ok," Amelia said. "We are trapped in here. I'm sorry I brought all of you down here. I didn't think it would end like this."

"We all wanted answers, Amelia," Genessa said.

"Yeah, at least I know what happened to my granddad," Trustin said.

"But if the government has its way, we won't remember any of this," Amelia said. "There has to be something we can do..."

"Your foolishness was always going to become a one-way trip, child," Janet said. "However you got down here, and whoever led you here, knew this was a one-way trip. There was never an escape of any kind."

Amelia looked Janet in her cold, brown eyes.

"You're right," Amelia said. "This *is* a one-way trip. You government officials were so greedy that you fed humans to an alien to prolong your lives. Us being down here was never about us at all. It was about the alien. It was always about the alien."

"You guys," Amelia said. "We need to shut down the spire."

Chapter 9

"Pardon??" Trustin said. His tone was thick with bewilderment. "Have you lost your mind?"

"No," Amelia said. "We were looking at it wrong the whole time. We came down here because we were driven by selfish motives. I wanted info about my dad. You wanted info about your grandfather. Asher and his brothers wanted to prove their value in the community. Genessa wanted to prove she's better than you and that she's a great friend."

"Excuse you," Genessa said. "I'm right here. I'm taking that as a compliment and an insult. So what now? Are we really shutting the spire down?"

"Yup," Amelia said.

"Are you just as stupid as your proxy friends?!" Janet said. "You don't know what will happen if you shut that down. Multiple layers of containment hold the L.I.C.H.

in place. Shutting that down is a death sentence for all of us!"

"And Brainwashing isn't?" Amelia said as she headed to the comp terminal. Abel and Eli followed.

"So what should we be looking for, guys?" Amelia asked.

"From the sounds of the recordings, they made the spiral because of the alien," Eli said.

"So we should be looking for something with the L.I.C.H protocols, I guess," Abel said.

"That makes sense," Amelia said. "Sorry, I got you guy wrapped in this."

"It's ok," Eli said. "This alien has been locked up for a really long time. I wonder if his family misses him?"

"Probably depends on how long his people live," Abel said. "Maybe he doesn't have any people left..." Eli and Abel's faces turned sour, but they still focused on their task.

BOOMBOOMBOOM

"Spokesperson McMurphy! Can you hear me?" Major Churchill's voice came through the internal speakers of the station.

"Yes, Major," Janet said. "I can hear you fine. These children are disrupting things and need to be stopped."

"We will be in the tunnel leading to Gamma station in 5 minutes." The Major

"Hurry, Major! They are trying to shut down the spire!"

"Roger that," Churchill said.

"Sounds like they're gaining access to the systems!" Trustin said.

"It's now or never, guys," Amelia says.

"It's now then," Abel said. He tapped on the tablet a few more times, and a whirring sound could be heard outside the station.

The spire was shutting down.

Amelia and Genessa went to the hatch to see the spire. One at a time, the lights on the outside went out until the spire went completely dark. Then a whir started to sound. The sound picked up speed. Amelia and Genessa went back to the comp terminal where the group was.

"You guys hear that?" Amelia asked.

"Yeah, that sound is picking up speed," Asher said.

"You idiots created a feedback loop! You didn't shut down the spire in the correct sequence!" Janet snapped.

"So what does that mean?" Trustin yells.

"I don't know!" Janet yells. "The last reported feedback loop happened before I was born!"

WWWRRRRRR… WWWRRRRRR… WWWRRRRRR…

WWWRRRRRR WWWRRRRRR WWWRRRRRR

WWWRRRRRR!WWWRRRRRR!WWWRRRRR!

A red light starts to shine on the spire. A screeching sound comes from the spire.

The group starts to scream and falls to their knees. Blood drips from their noses.

"AAAUUGGGGHHH!!! What is that?!" Trustin yells.

"It's coming from the alien!" Janet replied. She writhed in pain and held her ears.

A cascade of overloads happened, and small explosions could be heard. A kinetic wave of energy explodes from the spire and hits the Gamma station. The station rocked violently, throwing everyone to the ground. Amelia gets slammed into the wall and hits the ground. Everyone else started to pick themselves up, but Amelia and Trustin stayed down. They started to convulse.

"Amelia! Wake up!" Genessa yells.

"Get them to the medbay!" Asher said as the four of them dragged Amelia and Trustin to the medbay from the comp terminal. Janet used that time to access the comp terminal.

*****

Where am I Amelia thought to herself in the darkness. Then she saw that she blinked, but she didn't blink.

What am I looking at? Why can't I hear? She walked down some stairs, but she didn't walk down the stairs. She turned a corner at the bottom of the stairs to see a small humanoid being. It was about a meter tall. It had vertical, oval, black eyes. She couldn't see a pupil or iris. It had olive green skin and appeared to wear something that resembled a rain poncho. She reached out with her hand, but not her hand, and rubbed the head of this humanoid being. She saw that her arm had something that resembled a bracer. It had an intricate design and seemed to glow a warm hue of blue. It was almost paper-thin and was half the length of the ones she usually saw around school. The hand had three fingers. To be more accurate, two fingers and a thumb. The little one looked as if it had no mouth until it smiled from the head rub. Amelia noticed that she didn't feel anything when she rubbed its head, but she didn't rub its head.

In the blink of an eye, she was sitting in front of multiple screens. Six small screens on her left and six small screens on her right. They were relaying information that she couldn't understand. Some had lines and arcs that she only understood because of geometry class. She looked around, but she didn't look around, and saw that she was sitting in some kind of captain's chair. She thought it was odd that she couldn't see her legs, even though it looked like she was sitting down. There were lights, dials, and switches. The monitors to the left and right left a gap in the middle. There was a massive wall in front of her, but not in front of her; that was all black. It was about 4 meters in front of her and roughly 5 meters wide. It was three meters tall.

Why is this wall all black? She wondered to herself. Then it seemed as if the room moved, and a planet appeared on screen. A planet with a lot of green and blue. *Is that Earth?* She thought to herself. *No, those aren't the continents from Earth. The land is shaped differently. If that's land.* The planet moved away from the wall, and the wall started to move. It looked like she passed a moon, but she didn't pass a moon. And then the black wall started to show these cerulean blue and violet colored lines, as if she was moving through a tunnel very fast, but she wasn't moving through the tunnel very fast. She looked at one of the screens on her right. There was a yellowish circle on the monitor, and a green triangle in an arc that looked to intercept it.

In the blink of an eye, she saw smoke filling the room. Red lights flashed. She looked at a monitor to her left, but she didn't look at the monitor to her left. There was an isosceles triangle on it. It more or less looked like a Tower shell. The screen showed the Tower shell, with the point up. There was a red rectangle that covered the back left part of the shell. It looked like the shell had a hole. She whipped her neck, but not her neck, to look at a monitor on her right. She saw that the green triangle was about to collide with the yellow circle. She saw her hands, but not her hands, grip the chair's arms. The monitors collapsed onto the floor, and a green bubble encapsulated the chair. A liquid filled the space in an instant. The chair jostled and broke free of its moorings on the floor. Amelia saw herself, but not herself, fly toward the giant black wall.

In the blink of an eye, she was standing at an opening and walking down the stairs. It looked like she was wearing a space suit. She noticed that her legs, but not her legs, were shaped like a horse's. Her knees were facing behind her. She recognized the legs from history class. Her planet didn't have horses, but she thought they were a magnificent animal she hoped to meet one day.

She walked down the steps and turned around. She saw what looked like a giant Tower shell. She took a few steps back and looked at the entire structure. The structure looked about 15-20 meters long. The largest part was in the back. Amelia assumed that was where the engine or some kind of propulsion was. It looked to be 5 or 6 meters at the base.

The Tower shell had sustained significant damage. She looked at her bracer, but not her bracer, tapped it a few times, and a light shone from it. A purple light. She walked along the edge of the ship, and the purple light scanned it. She walked to the giant hole on the left, and the purple light began to flicker. It changed multiple colors and then shut off. It then showed some alien writing and a progress bar. It looked about 20% full.

Then Amelia walked closer to the hole and examined it. There was a rock the size of a bowling ball on the inside of the ship. She tapped on her bracer, but ot her bracer, and her ship seemed to push the rock out toward Amelia. She reached out with her gloved hands, but not her gloved hands, and examined it. It was black, with craters. She glanced back at the ship, and small pieces were slowly but surely moving inside. It looked like the ship was repairing itself. She looked again at the rock in her hands. There looked like something was oozing from it. She looked closer, and then she saw sparks and flashes of light from her peripheral vision. She dropped the rock, and it hit the ground with a thud. When she looked down, half the rock showed, forming a crater in the ground. She looked in the distance and saw a familiar shape. Humans. Humans with weapons.

In the blink of an eye, Amelia was in a town, surrounded by walls. These walls looked familiar to her.

She could tell that these eyes, not hers, were in a foreign place. The hands that were not hers swung at her side as she ran from building to street to building. Sometimes she jumped, covering distances that a human could only dream of under this gravity.

While mid jump, she was hit with something and knocked out of the sky. She was hit with a water hose. A fight ensued, and people jumped on her. She was lying on her stomach and struggled to get free. But something had happened. She could see cuts and lashes on her arm. She looked at her bracer, and it was no longer glowing. It looked like she started to vomit. *Am I sick?* Amelia wondered. She thought back to the recording. The recording that spoke about what happened when the alien touched humans. This was it. This was the fight with the Fire Brigade from the recording. *These humans were older and made me sick. That's how they were able to capture me,* Amelia thought to herself. The struggle stopped, and she pushed the bodies off with her hands, but not her hands. The entire Fire Brigade was dead. They looked to be shriveled up as if they had gone through severe dehydration.

In the blink of an eye, Amelia was inside a giant, circular room. Her spacesuit was tattered, and many scars and cuts on her body that wasn't her body. The room was bright with a lot of white light. There was barely enough room to stand and move around. Whenever she would stand, she collapsed to the ground. Something was wrong. She was hurt. Bad. The room lights turned a deep burnt ochre and started spinning above her head. The lights started flashing intermittently in apple green. The same green color on the signal bars. While lying on the ground, a hatch slid open. Humans started to walk in. One went to the right, then another went to the left. They were all in thin gowns and looked dead behind their eyes. Like they weren't themselves anymore, they didn't even acknowledge the alien that was in front of them. They just stared straight ahead. *Wait!* Amelia thought to herself. *I know these people!* Amelia saw them enter one by one. *This was the expedition from last year! This was...* And then she sees Bruce Dunne, Trustin's grandfather. And at the end of the group is Roger Butler, Amelia's father.

PAPA! CAN YOU HEAR ME? She screamed. But nothing came out of her mouth that wasn't her mouth.

"AMELIA! Wake up!" Genessa screamed.

What was that? Amelia thought. *Doesn't matter. Somehow, I need to get through to him!*

The expedition's members stood against the wall, their eyes soulless and unblinking. They lifted their hands in front of them and started to walk toward Amelia, but not Amelia.

No! Stop! Amelia tried to scream. She moved her arms, but not her arms, to wave them away. The expedition didn't acknowledge her existence.

"AMELIA, PLEASE WAKE UP!" Genessa sobbed.

Not now, Genessa! Amelia thought. She watched as the expedition started to cover her body, but not her body. She could see their faces shriek in pain, but she couldn't hear anything. Their skin began to stretch and become taut. She closed her eyes, but not her eyes. She didn't want to see their last moments.

Amelia's eyes opened wide as she gasped for air and flailed her limbs.

"Grab her before she hurts herself!" Trustin yelled.

Genessa, Asher, Abel, and Eli helped Trustin hold Amelia.

"Amelia, stop!" Genessa said.

"I-I can hear you," Amelia said as she started to come to her senses.

"You had me worried," Genessa said.

"What happened?" Amelia asked while leaning up on her elbows.

"Something hit the station really hard, and we all hit the ground. Then you and Trustin had seizures," Abel said.

Amelia looked at the group and saw hints of dried blood on their faces.

"Did everyone have nosebleeds?" Amelia asked.

"Yeah," Asher responded. "From the high-pitched blast that hit before the other blast hit."

"I'm confused," Amelia said.

"We all are," Trustin said. "I assume you heard the sounds, since you and I were the only ones who had seizures."

"What do you mean?"

Trustin proceeded to tell Amelia and the group that he heard voices when he was unconscious. A lot of clicks that sounded like speech, but a language he had never heard before. He also talked about alarms and explosions. Then he said he heard English. Humans yelled and fired their guns. Then water wooshed, and something was spinning. He heard a voice yell in a language he didn't know, and he woke up."

Amelia's eyes widened as she explained the visuals she saw matched with Trustin's sounds. She paused for a minute as her throat tightened. She told them about the last expedition, that she saw Trustin's grandfather and her dad. That they were out of it like zombies, and there wasn't anything she could do. The screaming Trustin heard was the alien trying to stop them because he didn't want to be touched.

"I'm sorry I couldn't stop it, Trustin," Amelia said. Tears streamed down her face. Trustin followed suit. He kneeled by her and hugged her."

"Thank you," Trustin said. "We all did our best."

"Wait... Where's my bracer?" Amelia asked while she stood up.

"The security came in while you guys were knocked out," Genessa said. "They locked us in here while they're handling the other issue." She pointed to the locked door to the medbay.

"What happened to Mrs. McMurphy?" Amelia asked.

“She’s helping out the officers,” Genessa said. “Apparently, the officers had gear that kept them from getting knocked around as hard as we did. Shutting down the spire really put them in a panic mode.”

“If they know what I know,” Amelia said. “I’d panic too.”

“What do you mean?” Trustin asked.

“Well, there’s an alien ship that's unaccounted for, and a giant black rock that had some tar-like liquid that oozed out of it. When the alien dropped it, it smashed into the ground so hard that it made a small crater. That rock seemed really heavy. If that alien is strong enough to hold that rock, I’m sure it's strong enough to –”

BOOM!

“There it is,” Amelia said with a smirk.

“What’s that? That doesn’t sound like shooting.” Asher said.

“Nope,” Amelia said. “Sounds like someone is about to make a grand entrance.”

BOOM!

BOOM! BOOM!

The sound of metal bending and breaking echoed in the cave. People started to yell, and the group heard the panicked shuffling of boots.

RRRAAAWWWWWWWRRRRRRR!!!!

They looked at each other with anxiety and excitement. They may not speak an alien language, but they knew what that sound meant.

The L.I.C.H. was free.

Chapter 10

Janet McMurphy's bottom lip trembled as she heard the screeching of metal from the spire. She ran to the front hatch of Gamma Station and saw with her own eyes a piece of the being she had drained power from. They made the spire to withstand an assault from the inside, but only if it had power. The L.I.C.H. stuck its hands out and pushed the hatch open somewhat. It peered through the gap and looked around. Janet could see it, but it couldn't see Janet.

Yet.

"Sound the Alarm!" Major Churchill screamed.

AHWWOOOOGGGAAAAHHHH

AHWWOOOOGGGAAAAHHHH

The klaxon blared so loud that the Major could barely shout orders.

The red alert lights bathed the stations in red. Janet McMurphy was typing commands at a feverish pitch at the comp terminal in the Gamma station.

"Reset the spire! Reinforce the hatches!" The Major yelled more orders.

BOOM!BOOM!

The L.I.C.H. could be heard kicking the hatch to the spire, which started to give way.

"The hatch to the spire is damaged!" Janet screamed. "The spire can't reset! Kill the thing!"

"A-Team in Beta station! B-Team in Delta station! Take your positions!" Major Churchill screamed.

A cacophony of boots started rushing to their positions.

"Major!" Janet screamed. "You can't use projectile weapons! If you hit any of the power sources for the spire, you'd blow us all up!"

"Your special counsel didn't brief us on the strengths and weaknesses of this thing!" Churchill yelled. "So you want it dead, but didn't tell us how to kill it. And turn off that freakin siren!"

"You'll have to use some kind of energy-based weapon," Janet said. You'll need to get it contained in the spire."

"You just told us to kill it! Now you want it recaptured? With the spire damaged, can it be recaptured?"

"Your men are more than capable of causing enough damage to subdue it at a minimum."

Meanwhile, the group listened as best they could above the klaxon.

"From the recordings we heard," Genessa said, "I don't think they have the weapons to hurt the alien."

"So what do we do?" Asher asked.

"We wait for an opening to get out of here," Trustin said. "I was able to feel what the alien felt. And right now, it's definitely feeling rage. It isn't going to go quietly. It will put up a fight."

"They do have the weapons to hurt the alien," Amelia said. "Remember that scientist on the recording? He said that the Fire Brigade died trying to stop the alien. But the alien was hurt because they were older. Look at the officers. Most of them are over Fifty. They have some wrinkles and some grey hair. Janet is hoping that they are going to come in contact with the alien and give their lives to weaken it."

"Why in the world would they come in contact with it?" Eli asked. "That's crazy!"

"I don't think the officers know," Amelia said. "Major Churchill said they haven't been briefed. So that means the spokespeople or whatever 'special counsel' Janet is with didn't tell the officers everything. They're willing to sacrifice more lives to still get to their end game of draining the life force out of this alien."

"This is really disgusting," Genessa said. "We need to stop this, but there isn't a way out of here."

"Not for us," Trustin said. "But there is for him. If we could pick up some kind of memories from the alien, then he's picked up memories from Amelia and me. He might have also picked up some memories from the officers out there. He knows something about these stations, and he's going to figure a way out of here. Then, in the commotion, we will make our move. For now, we need to hide." The group agreed and decided to stay near the back of the station, away from the fight.

"Switch your loadout," Major Churchill said. "This is CQC now!" The officers holster their pistols and equip shock gauntlets and electric rods. They opened the hatches to their respective stations and started walking toward the spire.

BOOM!

The hatch to the spire fell to the ground, and the alien stepped out. It covered its eyes from the station lights. As it stood up completely, the officers could see it was about 3 meters tall, olive-green, and wearing tattered rags. An electric hum was heard from the officers' gear as they moved toward the L.I.C.H. As its eyes adjusted to the light, the L.I.C.H. saw that it was under threat and took a step back.

"▫◻ ❒ ⍓◻⧫ ▫❒ ❍ " the L.I.C.H said.

As it started speaking to the officers, it put its hands palms facing outward, but no one understood what it was saying. It tried to maneuver from the spire's opening.

"It's moving away from the spire!" the officer yelled.

"Hold your ground, Windsor!" Major Churchill replied.

"It-it's coming at me! AAAAHHHH!" Windsor yelled and charged the L.I.C.H.

The L.I.C.H., a full meter taller than Windsor, instinctively reaches out and palms Windsor's face. The contact triggered an energy drain for both of them. The officers see that Windsor is hurt and rush to attack the L.I.C.H. More and more contact starts to drain them all. The officers' energy poisoned the L.I.C.H., and the L.I.C.H. drained them. It was a vicious cycle that the L.I.C.H. knew all too well, but could not explain to his current adversaries.

As the officers continue their attack, the L.I.C.H. pushes and throws them to gain some space to catch its breath. Wounds started to appear on its skin, and forest green blood dripped from its mouth. Before the next wave of assaults could begin, the L.I.C.H jumped toward the spire's broken hatch. It picked up the hatch and pitched it like a softball toward the Gamma station.

"Look out!" Janet screamed as the hatch flew vertically into Gamma Station. It smashed through the station hatch, causing significant damage to the comp terminal, and tore open the medbay, destroying the capsules in the process. The L.I.C.H. dashed for the opening in the Gamma station.

"After it!" Churchill yelled.

The officers were still gathering themselves together, not understanding the nature of their tiredness. With refocused determination, the officers continued their pursuit.

The L.I.C.H. made an amazing leap above the damaged hatch and onto Gamma Station. The opening was long and deep, but not wide. It started the difficult process of maneuvering itself down into the station, bit by bit. The metal scraped and sliced its already damaged skin, but the opening started to give way.

"A-Team," Major Churchill yelled, "Flank the left! B-Team, flank the right! Cromwell, Attlee, Pitt, on me!"

"Yes, sir!" the officers responded. A-team ran toward the Beta station hatch, and B-Team ran toward the Delta station hatch. Major Churchill took off his shock gloves to reveal a pair of fingerless gloves. As they ran toward Gamma Station, the L.I.C.H. struggled to get inside through the tear it caused. Major Churchill paused at a distance.

"Attlee, Pitt, give me a lift," he said. "Watch my six, Cromwell."

Attlee and Pitt ran to the edge of the damaged hatch, faced each other, and interlocked their hands.

Major Churchill sprinted toward his men and jumped into their interlocked hands. Attlee and Pitt launched Churchill up to the damaged opening, and he grabbed it. Once he braced himself, he waved Cromwell on, who followed suit. Churchill grabbed Cromwell's arm and helped him gain his footing. Churchill pulled out an FS knife from his utility belt and lunged toward the L.I.C.H. Churchill stabbed it in the thigh, and the L.I.C.H let out a roar of pain. The weight of both of them was enough to drop them into the Gamma station. Multiple floor panels buckled and bent from the force of the fall. Cromwell controlled his fall to land squarely on the floor next to the major and the L.I.C.H.

Janet McMurphy screamed in agony from underneath the broken floor. The L.I.C.H was pinned by the bent metal in the floor. It couldn't move its right arm, which was stuck inside the same compartment as Janet. The L.I.C.H, forced to touch Janet, began to drain her energy.

"NO!" She screamed. "Not like this!"

"The L.I.C.H. contorted its stabbed left thigh away from danger. It used its right leg to kick Churchill into Cromwell. As Janet was drained of energy, her screams faded into silence. The L.I.C.H. started to bleed more and cough up blood. It wiped its mouth, but for the first time, it looked defeated. Taking Janet's energy meant it had been poisoned. Its head bobbed up and down as it tried to remain conscious.

"Look!" Amelia said as she pointed at the L.I.C.H. "Ms. McMurphy stopped screaming." The gang slowly moved closer to the giant hole carved in the wall by the hatch door. The hole was big enough to get through, but it obviously wasn't safe to do so. Not yet.

"The recordings said that touching the alien is going to hurt us and it," Abel said. "It doesn't look so good." The group can see the alien has a hard time staying conscious. Over to their side of the station, they hear officers approaching.

"Don't touch it!" Amelia screams. "Touching it will hurt you!"

"Shut up, kid!" Churchill replied. "We have to kill this thing."

"Ms. McMurphy isn't screaming anymore," Genessa chimed in. "Look at its arm. It's underneath the paneling, touching Ms. McMurphy. We can't have physical contact with it."

Churchill and Cromwell paused and looked at each other. A-Team and B-Team entered through their respective hatches. Churchill gave a signal to hold position. The officers stared at the alien as its neck slumped down and its eyes closed.

"It looks dead," Attlee stated. "Is it still dangerous dead?"

"Assume yes," Cromwell replied. "Orders, sir?"

"We need to use some tools to move this thing," Churchill said. "With its arm trapped and Janet underneath, this isn't going to be easy. Sergeant, call Security. Tell them to bring down some pneumatic and welding tools. We are going to have to cut this Station up to get this thing out of here and back in the spire. Spokesperson McMurphy is, unfortunately, collateral damage."

"Yes, sir," Cromwell said and headed to the tram at Alpha Station. He started talking into his bracer and relayed info while he walked.

"No!" Trustin yelled. "You can't put it back! That spire is a torture chamber!"

"Shut up, kid," Churchill said. "You don't know what you're talking about."

"And you do?" Trustin snapped. "You idiots didn't know not to touch it. Ms. McMurphy hid the truth from you, but the information is on the bracers you took from us. If you hadn't damaged the comp terminal, you could've had more info on the alien. Listen to the audio files. They will tell you what's going on."

Major Churchill glared at Trustin. His knuckles were white from his tightened fist. He was being shown up in front of his men, and that didn't sit well with him. He inhaled sharply and motioned for Pitt to step forward.

"Give me a bracer for this brat to use," Churchill muttered.

Churchill walks over to the hole in the wall that opened into the medbay. Trustin walked to the opening and reached for the bracer, Amelia's bracer. Churchill slapped off Trustin's cap and grabbed him by the collar. He yanked Trustin mere centimeters from his face.

"Find the audio files on this bracer to prove what you're saying is true," Churchill said under his breath. "If you or your friends try anything funny or stupid with this bracer, I'll put a bullet in your forehead."

“Your threat is hollow, old man,” Trustin whispered. “You can’t hurt me. You know my father is a spokesperson.”

Trustin snatched the bracer, and Churchill shoved him back into the medbay. Trustin stumbled and fell but was otherwise unhurt. He put the bracer on and tapped it. He went to the files and played the proper audio. Churchill synced the bracer sound to the Gamma Station's internal speakers. The officers listened in stunned disbelief, dumbfounded that the spokespeople would keep this information from them. After they listened to some key recordings, the officers let the silence hang in the air.

“You guys are having the same reactions we had when we heard it,” Amelia said. “So, at least now you know what the alien is and how long it's been down here. But what isn’t mentioned in the older recordings is that the spokespeople are using the townsfolk to force-feed the alien citizens. Then they would siphon energy from the alien into these capsules. Or, what’s left of them. These capsules and the alien energy allowed the user to prolong their life.”

"Well, the answer to the situation is easier than I thought, then," the Major stated. "We have to kill this thing to protect the town."

"No!" Trustin yelled. "It's innocent in all of this! It didn't come down here to hurt us!"

"Yeah, I'm sure it didn't," Churchill replied. "But its existence puts everyone in danger. The spokespeople will keep up the lottery to feed off it. And my men are in danger of being 'replaced' because now we know what's actually down here. We can't let the townfolk know, because they could riot, and it could cause a civil war. And that's all because the people from 90-plus years ago didn't kill it when they should have. This entire energy drain program has killed hundreds, if not thousands, so that the spokespeople can abuse it. Putting it out of its misery would be a mercy."

"This isn't right!" Genessa screamed. "It shouldn't have to die because our ancestors didn't do right by it."

"You're right," Churchill agreed. "But it is what it is."

"Wait!" Amelia said. "We need to know who is in charge of this program and what they have planned. And we don't know what would happen if we killed it. You see what happened when the spire shut down. It created some kind of energy discharge. What if killing it created a cave-in? We could all get buried."

"Those are the breaks, kid," Churchill said. "Look, I can't let you go topside with the info you have. And I can't procrastinate on killing it. Look at it. It's not bleeding anymore. It's probably healing. You saw the way it threw the hatch door from the spire. It's insanely strong. We can't take this thing down in a physical fight. If we can't cut it up with the tools that Attlee brings back, and we can't kill it with bullets, we will have to trigger a cave-in to bury it."

"I don't think it's going to hurt us, Trustin said. "Amelia and I saw into its mind. It's some kind of scientist. It was in space, and an accident happened. It's not even supposed to be here. It has a family. There has to be another way."

Everyone can hear the tram locking with Alpha Station. Attlee was back with tools. The group looked at each other with blank expressions. They were out of answers.

"Think that through, kid," Churchill said. "If this thing healed and escaped, and we know it can't touch us, what happens when it gets topside? And if it's using human energy to live, what happens when it gets hungry? And if you've been locked up and tortured somewhere for 90 years, you think you're coming out of that torture the same person? I know I wouldn't be the same."

Attlee ran into Gamma Station, gasping for air.

"Sir, we have incoming!" Attlee said, exhausted from his sprint.

"Incoming?" Churchill said with a perplexed tone. "From where?"

"The sky, sir," Attlee said. "There's a giant fireball headed toward the town. If it impacts..."

"It's an invasion!" Churchill exclaimed. "Sound the alarm! Warn the town to evacuate!"

"The spokespeople did that, sir! I tried to contact you, but the signal was blocked!"

"This thing has friends! They've jammed comms! We have to get topside and assist with the evac efforts! Everybody out!"

The group runs to the hole in the medbay wall.

"Not you," Churchill stated as he pulled a pistol on the group. "You wanted to give information that could tear the town apart. My men have are vetted. They know how to keep a secret. You kids, are just another casualty of this thing."

"You can't leave us down here!" Trustin yelled. "My father –"

"Will be told you died a hero, trying to save Mrs. McMurphy from that thing," the Major said matter-of-factly. "You'll be fondly remembered. A-Team, B-Team, lock it down and head topside. Pitt and Cromwell set charges on the doors, openings, and on the spire. Set charges on all the stations. How long on the trams until we are out of range of the cave-in?"

"Four minutes, sir," Attlee said.

"Alright, set the charges for eight minutes," Churchill ordered. "We'll get topside, help with the evac, and when the explosion goes off, we'll have an alibi. Weeks will go by before the town digs everything out of the rubble.

"Yes, sir!" The officers replied.

The Major backed out of Gamma Station as the officers followed orders to rig the stations for detonation.

The group looked at each other in defeat. Tears started to form. There was no way out.

Chapter 11

KLI-KLANG!

KLI-KLANG!

The group hears the hatches to other stations getting locked. In the distance, they hear the trams moving away.

"Ok," Trustin said. "We know they're gone." He looks at the countdown he started on the bracer.

6:10

"We have 6 minutes to hide or get out of here!" Trusted said. His voice cracked as he tried to sound confident.

"There's only one way out," Amelia said. "We have to wake it up."

"Uh, how do you plan on doing that?" Genessa asked.

"I'm going to touch it," Amelia said.

"That's crazy!" Trustin exclaimed. "You'll die!"

"Maybe," Amelia said. "But I think it can keep its friends from destroying our town."

"What if it wakes up and goes on a murder spree?" Genessa asked.

"No," Eli said. "Remember the scientist from the audio clip? He said that various ages affect the alien differently. This might work."

"In about 5 minutes, I don't think it'll matter," Trustin said, as he looked at the bracer. "Grab some wires and blankets. We will pull you off the alien when this gets dangerous. Or, more dangerous. We don't have time to talk you out of this."

The group ran to the rooms in the back and started tying blankets around Amelia's legs. She walked through the opening in the wall and lay on the ground. She reached out and put her hand on the alien's hand. In an instant, she could feel the energy transfer out of her. She gritted her teeth and screamed under her breath. She broke out in a cold sweat and started getting tired. Its chest started to heave, and she could see that the wounds on its leg had healed. She closed her eyes, and her head drooped.

"She's passed out!" Trustin said. "Pull her back!"

The group pulled Amelia away from the alien.

"Oh no," Genessa said. "She doesn't look good."

"Let's get her to the back room," Trustin said.

The group rolled Amelia onto a blanket and dragged her into the medbay.

"Her breathing is really shallow," Genessa said. "This is a medbay. There has to be something we can do. Something we can use!"

3:41

"I don't know if we have time to look for anything," Eli said. He pointed at the alien. "We might have the alien to deal with."

The group looked at the alien. It was awake and looked at them with its black eyes. It pulled its arm out from underneath the metal plate and saw Janet McMurphy's dead body. It closed its eyes and looked away, covering the body back up with the metal plate. It stood up and took stock of its surroundings. Two small vertical slits opened in the middle of its face, and it closed its eyes.

"W-What's it doing?" Abel stammered.

"I don't know," Tustin said. "Is it smelling something?"

It started to run directly toward them. Shocked, they started to scream from the back room they were in. The alien reached up and yanked down the hex plate that led upstairs. They could hear it as it rummaged upstairs. It threw down the small mattresses from the bedrooms that held the comp terminals.

2:00

" ◆●● ■□⧫ ⧫❒⧫ ⌛□⧫ ●⧫⧫● □■⧫," the alien said.

"What'd it say!?" Genessa panicked.

"I don't know," Trustin said. "But we need to keep our distance. Cover yourselves with blankets to avoid touching it. We don't have much time before the explosion."

"What's it going to do when the explosion hits?" Eli asked.

The alien ran into the back room where the group was located. It saw they were scared and huddled in a corner. The alien returned with all three mattresses and threw them onto the group.

"⌛ ■❍ ⧫ □●❍❒ ■ ◆●● ●□," the alien said.

"I think it knows about the bombs," Trustin said.

"Did covering us with mattresses give it away?" Genessa said sarcastically.

"If I die in this explosion," Trustin said, "I promise to haunt you first."

"Looking forward to it," Genessa said flatly.

The group could hear the alien moving furniture into the back room. The ceramics and metal creaked against each other. The alien's frantic footsteps stomped as it ran back and forth, in and out of the room.

"Can you see what it's doing, Trustin?" Eli asked.

"It's putting a bunch of stuff in this room," Trustin said. "I think it's trying to cushion us from the explosion."

0:32

As the alien looked over its body and brushed off its tattered clothes, it jerked its head upward and stared toward the east, at the ceiling. It closed its eyes and reached out with its hand open.

"Now it's just looking at the ceiling," Trustin said.

"I think it's talking to its ship," Eli said. "None of these recordings said anything about what happened to the ship. If it's just the ship or it's an invasion, I think it's talking to somebody out there."

“ ⍓□⧫ □■ ♦ □⧫❒ ♦,” the alien said.

*****

The doors to the Alpha station tram opened, and Major Churhill and his officers ran out. They left the hidden foyer and took a special elevator up to the bottom floor of the main Security Borough building. They ran down a hallway and through a reinforced door into the building's common area. The klaxons blared as the unit assessed the inside of the building. The staff was armed but minimal. Churchill went to the closest staff member.

“Report!” Churchill yelled.

“Sir!” The staffer responded with a salute. “There is a hostile alien ship flying through the city! None of our weapons has any noticeable effect.”

“I heard there was a fireball from the sky!”

“Yes, Sir! It was when it hit atmo. It just looks like a cone shell now that it's not on fire. Even the damage from entering the atmosphere seems to be gone. It hasn’t caused any major damage to the town, but the citizens are panicked, and that has caused civilian casualties.”

“Where are the spokespeople?”

"They initiated DEFCON 2 and went into a bunker with key personnel. We don't have the security clearance to open the door to the bunker."

"We'll head outside and help coordinate safety protocols," Churchill said. He signaled his officers, and they all headed outside.

The officers looked up and saw the spiral-shaped ship. It circled parts of the town but focused primarily on the West side of the security Borough. While the officers watched, the ship paused in mid-air, turned west, and flew in that direction.

"Sir, the alien is in that direction!" Cromwell exclaimed.

"I know," Churchill responded.

The unit felt a rumble beneath their feet. The explosives triggered the cave-in as planned.

"Well," Churchill said. "We can't go back the way we came. Head to the garage, and we will drive there topside. We have to figure out a way to stop that ship."

"Sir, I think it's too late," Cromwell said.

*****

The explosion devastated the caves. All the trams were damaged, and each station had taken significant damage. Alpha, Gamma, and Epsilon stations were hit the worst. Sparks flew in some places because of shorts in the equipment. Small fires started to consume the little oxygen available in the cave.

"Is everyone ok?" Trustin asked. He started to cough from all the dust in the air. He pushed the debris off as best he could.

"Yeah," Genessa replied. "I think so. Amelia isn't doing any better, though."

"We are ok too," Asher said, as he and his brothers started to move the mattresses off themselves.

"Well, the alien protected us," Asher said. "So it must have an idea about how to get out of here. We need to find it and make sure we follow whatever it says to do."

While they pushed the mattresses off, a loud commotion came from the next room. They could hear the alien moan in pain, but it was still pushing debris around. As Trustin pushed, he could see that the door was blocked. He picked up a piece of metal and banged on the walls.

"Help!" Trustin yelled. "We need to get out of here. Our friend is hurt, and she needs help!" The entire group started to yell for help. Then they heard a bang on the north wall in front of them,

BANG

BANGBANGBANG

BANG

“I'm sure it's trying to tell us something,” Genessa said. “But we can’t wait for something we can’t understand to get us out of here.”

“We’ll do what we can,” Trustin said. “This cave-in won’t go unnoticed. I'm sure help is on the way.”

“Maybe we don’t want the help that’s on the way,” Asher said as he helped his brothers from under the mattresses. “We were warned and threatened multiple times by that officer. If he’s on the way, wouldn’t he be expecting dead bodies? His officers set the explosives.”

“We have to do something,” Genessa said. “Or Amelia is going to die. We should at least be trying to reach the alien.”

“We are trying to reach it,” Trustin said. “Sounds like it's trying to reach us, too.”

While the group tried to get out of the room, they could hear a rumble from the surface. It got louder and louder. The station started to shake violently.

"It's a second cave-in!" Trustin yelled. "Everyone, get back under the mattresses!"

As the group started to move, the debris by the door shifted. As the doorway cleared, a 2.5-meter-tall being stood before them. It was covered in a Vanta black material and had an oval head but no face.

"Th-That doesn't look familiar," Genessa said.

"Everyone get behind me," Trustin said. He thrust his hands out horizontally in a show of protection.

The being entered the room and stood tall. The oval mask seemed to melt away, revealing the familiar face of the olive green alien. It was in a space suit of some kind that covered its entire body. There were various designs on it, along with some pulsing lights. It reached out to them with its covered hand.

"□○ ◆♦ ○ ▫ ❒ ♦ ■□◆," The alien said.

Trustin reached out and touched its hand. Nothing happened.

"It looks safe," Trustin said. Then he pulled on the alien's finger and brought it to Amelia. She was still unconscious and had a raspy breathing pattern.

The alien reached out with its right hand, palm open. The material of the suit swirled, and a device started to show in the palm of the alien's hand. It pointed the device at Amelia, and an orange light emanated from it. The group watched as Amelia's breathing started to regulate. After a few moments, she opened her eyes.

"Wh-What happened?" Amelia asked as she shielded her eyes from the orange light.

"You healed the alien," Genessa said. "And it saved us." She went to her friend and hugged her.

The alien shut down the device and stood up. It signaled them to follow. It guided them out of the back room and past all of the debris. It looked like a circular tunnel had been cut through the length of the station. There was an opaque material that created the tunnel. The tunnel led to a bright yellowish light. They followed the alien past the light. When their eyes adjusted, they realized they were on the alien's ship, and it used something to carve that tunnel.

"WOW!" Eli exclaimed. "This is amazing." The group looked around, and the door to the ship closed. They looked at the giant viewscreen while the alien sat in the chair with all the monitors. The ship lifted up out of the hole and went several hundred meters into the air. It started flying east back toward the town.

"This is the ship I saw in space this whole time," Eli said. "It waited for its friend."

"This can't be the same ship," Genessa said. "I thought Amelia said it had a hole in it."

"It did," Amelia said. "But it looked like it was able to fix itself. If it could fix itself, maybe it's the same ship. And being in space, it could scan for its friend."

"It waited for over ninety years?" Asher asked. "That's a long time."

"Maybe it's not a long time to the alien," Eli said as he stared in awe at the inside of the ship.

"Look, it's headed to town," Trustin said. They all gathered around the monitor. It showed the direction they were headed and the 2-D outline of the town to the east.

"□□♦ ❒ ♦❒□♦♦ ●□ ❍⍓ ●❒■," the alien chuckled. It moved the flat monitor toward the group so they could take a better look. It pointed at various monitors and told them what they did. The group didn't understand the language, but they understood enough of it. They were not in danger.

Trustin tapped Amelia on the shoulder and handed her the bracer.

"I think this belongs to you," Trustin said.

"Thanks," Amelia replied. "I guess my dad saved the day."

"The good ones usually do," Trustin said.

When it reached the admin building, it set up a force field around the ship in the form of a vertical tunnel. Various groups of citizens came out to gape at the spaceship. The ship landed in the street, and the alien let down the ramp. The group walked down the ramp one at a time. They said their various 'Thank Yous' and waved bye to the alien. As Amelia started to walk down the ramp to the waiting crowd, the alien touched her on the shoulder. She turned around to look at it. The mask came off its face, and they looked each other in the eyes.

"❄■□ ⍓□⧫, Sweetpea," The alien said.

Tears started to stream down Amelia's face as she turned and walked down the ramp. When the group was clear, the ramp pulled up to the ship, the door closed, and the ship started to rise into the sky. Once it was safe enough, the alien ship flew into outer space.

"Bye, Papa," Amelia whispered.

Epilogue

Diana walked over to the couch where Amelia patiently waited. She brought her purple moisturizer with her. It had been a month since the event in the West Woods, and she knew she couldn't put off talking about it any longer. She positioned herself on the couch while Amelia remained on the floor, and they started their usual tradition.

"You know," Diana started. "I didn't know about that deal your dad struck with the spokespeople. They gave me the bracer from your dad after one year like he requested. I don't think they knew it would be their downfall."

"I figured," Amelia said. "Most of it happened the way he said it would. It mostly worked out."

"So, do you and your friends finally have all the reports and debriefs done?" Diana asked.

"Yes, Madam Spokesperson," Amelia teased. "Everything seems to be accounted for."

"Well, I'm just filling in temporarily," Diana said. "I don't know if politics is really for me. I'm just glad you all are home safe."

"Some of us are," Amelia said in a mournful tone.

"What happened, Sweetpea?" Diana asked as she put some purple moisturizer in a tuft of Amelia's hair.

"With Trustin's dad in jail, he inherited the MeatPacking Borough. I don't think he wanted that responsibility this early in his life. It's a lot to manage. He was talking about the accelerated classes he has to take and the university courses to make sure he knows how to balance the political and business end of the Borough."

Yeah, it's a lot, especially for him and what he just went through. I didn't agree with it, but I was outvoted. I did make sure he could see his mom again, though."

"I knew you would handle that part. I don't think the town knows what to do with all the people from the psych ward. The news said almost 50% of them shouldn't be there, and new information from the special counsel servers is still showing how many people were framed. Ms. Siobhan didn't deserve that.

She was trying to help everyone see what was going on underground with the alien, but Mr. Edward just dismissed her and lied about her. That's just crazy to me."

Diana started on her second braid. She grabbed another bunch of hair that she had separated earlier.

"Power does that to people. The doctors and scientists are still wondering what the long-term effects of the alien's energy will be on those who used those capsules. They have to stay quarantined, even in jail. There's only so much info they can get from the damaged capsules. I hate that Churchill and his goon squad planted those explosives. Over 50% of the zygotes that were preserved in Epsilon Station were lost. I'm glad the proxy kids found out where they came from, though. Parliament agreed to reinitiate the original Proximus Protocols, so that's a good thing. There have already been over 30 successful pregnancies. I didn't think the town would be this excited, but after learning about all the atrocities, I think we just collectively want to make amends."

"Genessa is still staying with Morgan. Good thing, too, since her dad was caught up in everything. I'm glad

Tron House was turned into a makeshift museum about where they come from. I didn't know it was illegal for them to change their names if they were never adopted. Since they all got adopted, it'll be weird seeing their new names at school. It's going to take a long time to heal from this one."

"We have to trust each other, Sweetpea. We need to make sure we learn from our mistakes and move forward from there."

"Speaking of moving forward, I wonder what happened to our alien friend? Or even that giant black rock..."

"Right now, we can focus on the things in front of us. We can save those mysteries for another time."

www.ingramcontent.com/pod-product-compliance
Lightning Source LLC
La Vergne TN
LVHW020718110826
845149LV00012B/2319
9798998938122